HIDING GLADYS

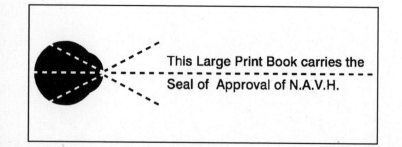

This Large Print Book carries the
Seal of Approval of N.A.V.H.

A CLEO COOPER MYSTERY

HIDING GLADYS

LEE MIMS

THORNDIKE PRESS
A part of Gale, Cengage Learning

Detroit • New York • San Francisco • New Haven, Conn • Waterville, Maine • London

GALE
CENGAGE Learning®

LIBRARY OF CONGRESS CATALOGING-IN-PUBLICATION DATA

Mims, Lee, 1948–
   Hiding Gladys : a Cleo Cooper mystery / by Lee Mims. — Large print edition.
      pages ; cm. — (Thorndike Press large print mystery)
   ISBN-13: 978-1-4104-6042-4 (hardcover)
   ISBN-10: 1-4104-6042-8 (hardcover)
   1. Large type books. I. Title.
PS3613.I591995H53 2013b
813'.6—dc23   2013015181

Published in 2013 by arrangement with Midnight Ink, an imprint of Llewellyn Publications, Woodbury, MN 55125-2989 USA.

Printed in the United States of America
1 2 3 4 5 6 7 17 16 15 14 13

For my family, with love.

Here about the beach I wandere'd, nour-
ishing a youth sublime
With the fairy tales of science, and the
long results of Time.

— Alfred Lord Tennyson

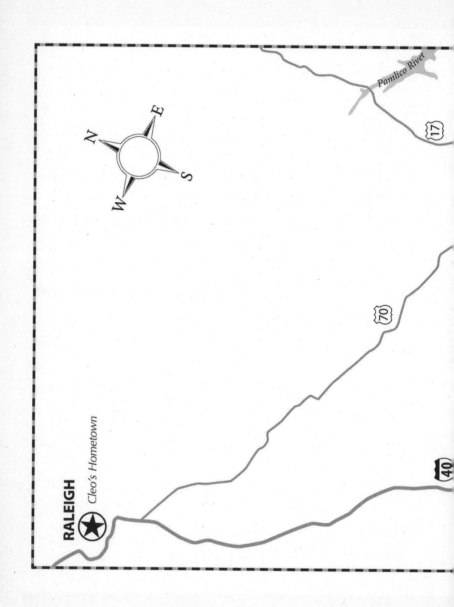

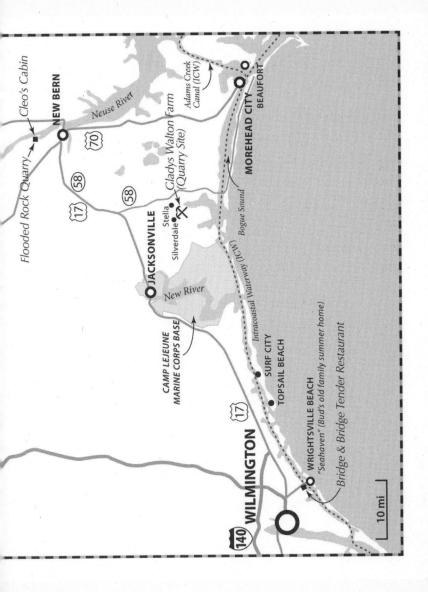

Cleo's Cabin

Flooded Rock Quarry

NEW BERN

Neuse River

{70}

{58}

{17}

{58}

Adams Creek Canal (ICW)

MOREHEAD CITY

BEAUFORT

Gladys Walton Farm (Quarry Site)

Stella

Silverdale

JACKSONVILLE

Bogue Sound

Intracoastal Waterway (ICW)

New River

CAMP LEJEUNE MARINE CORPS BASE

SURF CITY

TOPSAIL BEACH

WRIGHTSVILLE BEACH
"Seahaven" (Bud's old family summer home)

Bridge & Bridge Tender Restaurant

WILMINGTON

{140}

{17}

10 mi

ONE

Did you know that rattlesnakes don't rattle? They buzz, actually. Sounds like an angry hornet in a jar. Now, I'm a field geologist and have had some real-life experience with these nasty-tempered creatures, so you can imagine my concern when I thought I heard one while tooling down Highway 70 east in North Carolina at seventy-five miles an hour.

Though I was inclined to believe my imagination was being fueled by a large Mickey D's iced caramel coffee, I muted Stevie Ray Vaughan on the classic rock channel anyway and listened intently. Hearing nothing, I turned the music back on, glanced up to the rearview mirror, and got absolute confirmation that my day had just taken a decidedly bad turn.

Slithering along the top of the backseat was an eastern diamond-back, flicking its tongue, menacing, outraged at being in

11

unfamiliar surroundings. Every muscle in my body tensed — a good thing, or Id have wet my pants. Yet, frozen with fear as I was, I was still at the wheel of a moving car. Behind me, a horn blared. Jerking back into my lane, I overcorrected. My tires dropped off the right side of the pavement and roiled a trail of dust and road debris until I regained control.

I began to brake and looked back at the rearview.

The snake was gone.

Just then, Tulip, the sweet young deer-hound who'd recently adopted me, stood up in the cargo area and sniffed the air. A forty-pound dog ricocheting about inside the Jeep slinging a rattler in her jaws . . . not good. Nervous sweat dripped down between my breasts even as the conditioner blasted frigid air in my face. Worse, little black dots were floating before my eyes.

Perfect. I was going to pass out.

Calm down. Breathe. To survive this, I needed a plan. At that very moment, my uninvited passenger came up with his own, sticking his head out from under the seat right between my feet. Forget calm: I shrieked like a banshee, popped my seat-belt, and jerked my legs up under me. Sitting on my feet and still screaming, I held on for dear life as the Jeep careened down the wide shoulder of the raised roadbed.

With a jaw-slamming jolt, the vehicle dropped into a drainage ditch and slid forward, spewing mud, grass, and last year's cattails like slush from a snowplow until everything came to an abrupt halt.

Everything but me, that is. Sans seatbelt, I flew across the car, crashed into the space between the dash and the windshield, then bounced headfirst back on the passenger seat.

For a moment, the world stopped. There was dead silence. Next thing I knew, I was breaking land-speed records in an open-field dash through soybeans. Tulip streaked past me like a black and tan missile. About mid-field I stopped to gasp for breath.

Slowly, things started coming back into focus as I heard the mechanical buzzing of cicadas in the dense woods beside the bean field and felt the intense rays of the July sun beat down on my back. Tulip's tags tinkled merrily as she bounded back to me and sat at my feet. I stroked her bony head, straightened up, and stomped back between the lush rows of hip-high plants to the edge of the field.

The sight of my beloved Jeep covered in

muck and grass was enough to make me want to sit right down and cry. It looked like a wounded beast that had given up a long struggle to extricate itself from some tar pit and now lay waiting to die.

Where was my purse? In the Jeep, of course. Traffic whizzed by me as I warily crept up on the vehicle like . . . well, like it had a rattlesnake in it. Then I had a thought and patted the back pocket of my jeans. *Thank you, Jesus.* Instead of putting my cell phone in my purse, I'd shoved it in my back pocket, my new attempt to curb the bad habit of talking while driving. I pulled it out and checked to see if it had been damaged in the melee. It hadn't.

Flipping it open, I grimaced, rolled my eyes even, but there was nothing else I could do. I had to call my ex-husband for help. Yes, I could have called the roadside service my insurance provided, but I needed help now, and I suspected there was a good chance Bud was on this very highway headed home to Raleigh from the North Carolina coast. He always waited until Monday mornings to return, wanting to avoid Sunday traffic.

He answered immediately. "Cleo, babe," he chirped. "What a pleasant surprise."

Bad as I hated it, I said, "Hey, Bud? Are

14

you on the way back from the coast by any chance?"

"Yeah. You sound funny. You okay?"

"I'm fine. I just need a little assistance . . . getting out of a ditch."

"Ditch! What happened? Where are you?"

Just the macho overreaction I'd expected. "Calm down," I said and gave him my location.

Tulip and I were just settling down under a pine tree at the edge of the field to wait for Bud when the sound of a vehicle braking got my attention. I looked up and saw a black Ford Explorer pull onto the shoulder of the highway then back up, firing a hail of gravel against its undercarriage.

I stood, holding tightly to Tulip's collar. Even before I could read the vanity license plate — ROCK MAN — I knew who it was. My heart started pounding again, but this time it felt good.

Nash Finley climbed out of the black SUV and hurried over. His Attire — khakis, polo shirt, and Doc Martens — made it obvious he wasn't doing field work. I wondered what he was doing down east.

"Oh my gosh, it is you," Nash said, concern showing in his face. "I saw the Jeep in the ditch and thought it might be yours.

Glad to see you're okay." Then his face broke into a large grin. "I know you didn't drive off the road because you were putting on eye liner. What happened?"

"Nothing I can't handle," I replied sweetly.

Raising an eyebrow, Nash looked at the Jeep then back at me and tried again. "Seriously, Cleo, what happened?" He bent and scratched Tulip behind the ears. She returned his attention with a lukewarm tail wag.

"I'm not real sure." I wasn't sure why I was lying to Nash, except that I've learned the hard way not to give another geologist unnecessary information. Any talk of how a snake came to be in my car would naturally lead to where I'd been and what I'd been doing, and that was definitely not something I wanted to discuss — especially with the clever Mr. Finley. Nash worked for a small independent quarrying operation in the western part of North Carolina. I'd met him there over a year ago when that company hired me as an acquisitions consultant.

I was divorced at the time and had been for four years, but my heart was still bruised. Besides being very smart, Nash was funny and lighthearted, the kind of guy who makes you feel special. When my consulting gig ended, he'd come to Raleigh a few times

16

and we'd had dinner. I wanted to get to know him better, but then he stopped calling. I'd wondered why and still did, thinking maybe it had been the distance.

"Long time, no see," I said, forcing a casual tone. "What have you been up to lately?"

"Haven't you heard, sweet pea? I'm working for GeoTech now. Sales."

That explained the attire, but it still came as a surprise. GeoTech was the company I'd worked for before I left to start my own consulting business. I said, "Really? Hung up your rock hammer for good, did you?"

"Yeah," he said. "More money in sales. Right now, however, I'm interested in rescuing you." He stepped closer and rubbed my back in comforting little circles. "Maybe you fell asleep."

I felt my shoulders relax a little. A slight hint of Hugo Boss cologne floated on the humid air. "You never know . . ." I murmured, leaning into his warm hand. I was feeling a bit cold now that the adrenaline jolt had worn off.

"Let me call triple A," Nash said, pulling out his cell. "Then I'll get you right home and make you a drink. You look like you could definitely use one."

Oh shit. Bud. He was already on his way,

17

and there wasn't a chance in hell I could call and get him to carry on with his day. "Really, Nash," I stammered. "I can take care of —"

The blaring horn of a white pickup drowned me out as it roared past us heading west. I turned to watch my ex-husband flash his brake lights and left-hand blinker.

I looked back at Nash. "So how did I get lucky enough to have you happen by right now?"

Nash tracked Bud's progress as he slowed for a crossover about half a mile up. Then, turning to me, he said, "I'm headed to a couple of the down-east quarries, just checking on supplies, making sure all my contracts can be met. You know, the usual."

"Well, I appreciate your stopping, but I'd already called Bud and . . . you know how he is," I said lamely.

The truth was, how could Nash *not* remember? Bud had a habit of "just happening" to drop by the same restaurant in Raleigh where Nash and I were dining. Either he had a network of spies or else had managed to slip a homing device into my Jeep. But you have to admit it would be a pretty advanced tracer that would know to locate me only when my companion was male.

"Yeah, I remember," Nash said. Then, offering me another grin — an apologetic one this time — he turned to leave. Giving a little wave, he climbed into his SUV. "You're in good hands," he assured me and roared off just as Bud whipped across the grass median at one of those places reserved for Highway Patrol and emergency vehicles.

"Oh, shut up," I said to Tulip, still holding tightly to her collar as she strained to run to Bud. The mere sight of him generally sent her into quivers of delight. She whimpered and gave a dry hack as I pulled her down on her haunches.

My ex-husband, Franklin Donovan Cooper IV — ever grateful to have been nicknamed Bud — climbed out of his 4x4 Chevy and strode purposefully toward me.

"What was that jerk doing here?" he demanded.

"I'm fine," I said. "Good of you to ask, though."

"Oh. Sorry." He squatted to pat my wiggling hound. "You okay, Tulip?" Then he straightened, looked over at my Jeep, and said, "What the hell happened? And, again, what was that jerk doing here?"

"Obviously, I lost control," I said testily. "And Nash isn't a jerk. He just happened to pass by on his way down east. He's working in Raleigh now."

"Uh-huh," Bud said, then turned his attention back to my sorry-looking vehicle.

I followed him for a few steps, then stopped and called out, "And before you go any closer, where's your Glock?"

"In my truck. Why? Where's your baby nine?"

"Still in there with the rattler," I said, referring to my Glock 9mm. In case you're wondering, I carry a gun because my workplace is the great outdoors. Bud carries a gun because besides being an enthusiast, he's an Eagle Scout. Always prepared.

Bud stopped in his tracks and backed up a few steps. "Rattler?"

"Yeah."

He executed a quick about-face and walked back to me. "You want to start at the beginning, Cleo?"

"Well, I was heading to Gladys Walton's house to make sure she knows what to expect when the drill crew comes in next week and . . ." I stopped at the look of confusion on his face. "What?"

"Who's Gladys?"

If I'd been a cartoon character, my head would have inflated like a balloon and steam would have geysered out of my ears. "You see?" I said. "This is why we aren't married

20

anymore. No matter how many times I tell you what I'm doing, you don't seem to remember. Could it be that what I do is of no importance to you?"

"Could it be that you don't do anything that's all that important? Anyway, since you barely make enough money to keep body and soul together, this . . . this private consulting business of yours" — he said it like it was a disease — "shouldn't be important to you either."

Hands on hips, I glared at Bud. He glared back at me. Finally, he sighed and said, "What do you say we skip the oldies but goodies. Just tell me how a damn snake got in your car."

"Fine." I crossed my arms over my chest, regained my composure, and continued. "Honestly, I don't have a clue how it got in there."

Bud pondered the question only about two seconds, then said, "Well, considering all the places you take that Jeep, it probably just crawled in. Where have you been today? Besides this Gladys person's house."

My eyes narrowed and I squeezed my lips together until I had control of my words. "I haven't *been* to her house yet, and just for the record, she owns the land I have an option on. I was headed there to prepare for test drilling. The only place I've parked since last night is my house and McDonald's in Goldsboro this morning. I was only inside a few minutes."

"Did you lock the doors?"

"Probably," I said, looking to the clouds for clarity. "But just as probably not," I conceded.

Bud was quiet for a few moments as he stared at the Jeep, chewing the inside of his cheek — an irritating habit I shouldn't have to put up with anymore. Then he pointed. "Whoa! Looks like that snake's feeling right at home."

I looked and sure enough there was the rattler, stretched out on the dash enjoying a little sunbath.

"Bud. Are you going to help me out here or not? I'm kind of pressed for time."

He looked at me, tilting his head. "You going to feed me dinner tonight?"

"Sure," I said without a trace of guilt, despite the fact that I knew I wouldn't be back home in Raleigh for several days.

"You throwing in some dessert too?" He asked as he slipped an arm around my waist and leaned in to nuzzle his nose behind my ear. "I mean, it is a rattlesnake . . ."

I pushed him away, giving the same little smile that was second nature after twenty years of marriage. It committed me to nothing. It left the door open, though, and okay, I know — that was bad. So was the fact that since our divorce was finalized almost five years ago, we've both slipped up and slid back together from time to time.

But in my defense, old habits are hard to break and I was very young when I married Bud, only twenty years old. I'm forty-five now, but that doesn't mean I'm not human. Moreover, every time a slip-up has happened, some type of unusual situation was involved. And I've been very stern with myself afterward and made stronger resolutions never to let it happen again. And seriously, no way was I was going to deal with a rattlesnake on my own if I didn't have to.

Apparently Bud took my smile to mean a maybe because he slapped his palms together, gave them a little rub, and said, "Alrighty then. Let's get you on your way."

Two

In less time than it takes me to make a pot of coffee, Bud got the snake out of the Jeep and the Jeep out of the ditch. He just opened the passenger door and slapped the windshield a couple of times. I held tightly to Tulip's collar as the intruder slithered out and into the grass. Then Bud chained the Jeep to his truck and I steered while he pulled me out.

Well, he definitely wasn't getting dessert for something *that* easy.

A quick good-bye wave and I was off again. My Jeep now resembled a camouflaged combat helmet with clumps of broom straw and black mud covering it, but it still ran. I'd deal with the mess later.

Little over an hour later, after leaving Highway 70 for 58, I turned onto Morristown Road, then Wetherington Landing Road, heading deeper and deeper into lowland farming country in On-slow

County. I passed through the town of Stella and took a right onto Belgrade Swansboro Road before reaching the settlement of Silverdale, then navigated a few more back-country roads. Finally I reached Gladys's five-hundred-acre farm. A little research had revealed that the old two-story farmhouse was once the hub of an even larger working farm back in the early 1930s. Though Gladys kept the house in fairly good condition, it would need a ton of upgrades and renovation to make it marketable. Marketability wasn't a concern for Gladys, however. She was in her seventies and planned to use the money she'd get from me to set herself up in a very nice assisted-living facility.

Shutting off the engine, I noticed that neither her car nor her housekeeper's, who cleaned daily, was in its usual place. *Should I come back later?* I decided to soldier on. I wanted to get this show on the road. After all, I'd waited a lifetime for a geological break like this and now my ship was finally coming in.

There being no doorbell, I tapped the heavy pine door with the brass knocker. No one answered. I tapped again, humming an impatient little tune. A gentle breeze ruffled the leaves in the old oaks that overhung the wide porch but gave little relief from the stifling July heat. Just as I lifted the knocker to tap louder, the door flew open, making me jump like a startled rabbit. Standing in his socked feet — explaining why I hadn't heard his approach — was Gladys's thirty-four-year-old, live-in son, Robert Earle.

He was resplendent in plaid boxers, a sweat-stained wife beater, and a buzz-cut. Tattoos wiggled on his biceps as he braced his arm against the door. I knew that his pumped-up physique wasn't the result of manual labor that might have done him some good and made him a little money, but rather the result of his hobby: pumping weights recreationally. I curbed the impulse to tilt my head down to the spot where his gaze had come to rest: my breasts.

"Hi, Robert Earle, is your —"

"What the fuck are you doing here?"

Though he'd never been even the tiniest bit friendly, such flat-out rudeness almost threw me off my game. Almost. I said pleasantly, "I'm here to see your mother. Is she here?"

"No, she's not," he snapped, taking a step back to close the door. "Now get lost."

"May I ask where she is?"

"Are you deaf, retarded, or what?"

"Look," I said, ditching Miss Manners, "I

don't give a rat's ass what you think of me, but your mother, besides being a friend, is also a business partner of mine."

"What kinda business partner?" said Shirley, who'd now come up behind her brother. She was also a thirty-something, live-at-home adult. Her plain face was less than enhanced by the heavy-framed glasses and the trench they'd worn into the bridge of her nose. She adjusted the specs with her index finger and sneered, "She didn't mention any partnership to me."

"Be that as it may," I said with commendable patience, "I have a signed option to test this property, all nice and legal, and I intend to do just that starting next week. I wanted to speak to your mother about what to expect once the drill crew's here."

Robert Earle's eyes bulged and I saw the tendons working across his jawbone. His fists clenched. Apparently alarmed, Shirley put her hand on his bunched biceps. "Now, Robert Earle . . ." She didn't get any further.

"You've got nothing of the kind. Now get off this porch before I toss your fancy butt over that railing."

He was dead wrong, of course, but I had no desire to be tossed into the sticker bushes. So undignified. I backed up a step and said, "Tell your mother I'll be by in the morning to see her."

Somehow I managed to affect a leisurely stroll to my Jeep. Well, my fancy butt may have been the tiniest bit tucked. Tulip let out a low growl as I slid behind the wheel. One thing about my new hound, she knew a varmint when she saw one.

"Good girl!" I told her. Waving cheerfully, I headed down the drive. At the intersection with the main farm road, I stopped. *Who else might know where Gladys is?* One person came instantly to mind. I turned right and headed her way.

Patches of sunlight dappled the dirt path that led to a modest 1950s cinder-block tenant house on a corner of Gladys's farm. I steered carefully between pines and pin oaks and thought back to a conversation I'd had with Gladys one morning when she told me that Irene Mizzell wasn't really a housekeeper.

She was, in fact, Gladys's first cousin. When Irene's husband, a shrimper from Harker's Island, passed away, Gladys had offered her the tenant house and some money to tide her over until she got a job. Chuckling, Gladys had told me how the first morning after Irene moved to the farm, she'd turned up in Gladys's kitchen, mak-

28

ing breakfast. Irene had been cooking, cleaning, and helping with the chores ever since. I searched my memory for how long ago Gladys had said that was . . . maybe twenty years.

My knock on the front door of Irene's house startled a barn swallow out of the mud nest she'd built in the corner of the green and white aluminum awning over my head. I looked around the prim little yard. I was sure the Honda Accord parked in the dirt drive was Irene's. Everything was neat as a pin. Bedding plants bloomed in front of a low hedge of compacta holly. Three hummingbirds battled for the meager drops of sugar water left in the feeder hanging from a window awning that matched the one over the stoop.

How long did it take for birds to empty a feeder? Hours? Days? I'd met Irene a few times and she didn't seem to be one to let her feeders run low. I knocked on the door again, paused a beat, then walked over to a picture window and peered in.

What I saw was just your average modest little den, with a La-Z-Boy facing a portable television that sported rabbit ears and a jarringly modern converter box. The recliner was topped by an afghan crocheted in a zigzag pattern that faded from deep maroon to pale pink. I walked around to the back of the house, looked in a few more windows, and checked the back door.

It was locked too. Well, hell, it was a good idea to try Irene, but it really didn't matter that she wasn't here, maybe off for a walk. Gladys was bound to be home tomorrow. I had plenty to do in the meantime.

Tulip and I got back in the Jeep and headed for the back of the property to start laying a grid for testing.

THREE

By the time I got to the site it was nearly two o'clock and I hadn't eaten any lunch. I felt around in my field bag and came up with a pack of Nekot cookies and a bottle of water. Peanut butter for protein. Sugar for energy. What more could a girl want? I wolfed down a couple cookies then opened the cargo door for Tulip. She leapt out and took off for the woods at the edge of the open pasture. I waited until she dove into the thick underbrush, then whistled her back.

Like magic she was at my side. I gave her half a cookie just to reinforce rules she'd apparently never understood. Come when you're called so you don't end up abandoned in the woods by a feckless owner with a whole kennel full of hunting dogs just like you. "Aw, no one could be just like you, girl," I said, giving voice to my thoughts. I gave her ear a playful tug and sent her off again.

Finishing my lunch, I took in the base line of surveyor's flags I'd staked out on a quick trip last week. The row stretched across the 150-acre pasture, flags set at intervals of two hundred feet. I hadn't seen Gladys then either. Actually I'd tried to call her several times over the last two weeks, but she hadn't answered. Still, I wasn't worried, I had only wanted to give her specifics on the testing and let her share in the excitement. She already knew everything she needed to know: initial testing would take about two weeks and the option she had signed allowed me to conduct this testing to confirm that rock of marketable quality and in sufficient quantity was present. She'd been raring to go.

A soft gust of wind passed and the little three-inch, orange plastic flags vibrated merrily on their wire stems. I needed to place additional rows of flags parallel to my base line. Once the drill crew got on site, they'd drill a hole at each flag. Data from these holes would tell me the number of feet to the top of the rock. Assuming the rock was there, of course, although all my instincts and prior field work told me it was.

In fact, I was relying heavily on my instincts and only somewhat on field indicators. But that didn't matter. I could feel it in my bones: the rock was there.

Very hard rock, the kind of rock used in almost every kind of construction on the planet, lay just under my feet. The most important thing to know, however, was where my feet were planted. This location was very rare indeed for this type of rock. If my predictions were right — and I was betting every dime in my savings account they were — I had found the easternmost deposit of granite in the United States.

It didn't matter that no major construction or new highway was scheduled nearby — my usual prerequisite for prospecting — I was close enough to Morehead City, a major port, to move the stone anywhere it needed to go up and down the East Coast.

A jolt of electricity shot through me at the notion of everything this meant. Certainly money. But fame too. In geologic circles anyway. I could already see my name in boldface on important scientific papers in prestigious journals.

Hours later, I had covered about half of the field, working my lines back and forth from the edge of the pasture to a creek deep into the woods. At one point as I reached the edge of the pasture, I heard Tulip crashing through the trees beyond me. Probably chasing a squirrel. I flagged the last drill hole on the line, then stepped back into the woods and whistled for her. More crashing about let me know she was down by the broad, shallow creek that fed off the White Oak River and ran through the back portion of Gladys's farm.

I pushed my way downhill through greenbriars and honeysuckle, following the sound of her barking. She was standing on her hind legs, front paws on a massive pine trunk, looking up into the branches, letting me know she'd done her job. She treed something.

Placing my pinky fingers between my lips, I curled my tongue and let out a shrill whistle that caught her attention. "Tulip!" I called. "Get over here, girl!"

She stubbornly didn't respond, so I walked over and looked up into the tree. A squirrel scolded me from high in the branches. "Good girl," I said, giving her a pat. Then I moseyed over to the creek bank and looked down at the water, gurgling and swirling about three feet below me. Here was some of the highest ground on the farm, and actually the place I'd first seen the outcrop of in-place granite. The rock lay exposed under an unusual twist of pine tree roots and was just barely visible. I'd never even have spotted it had I not stepped in the creek to retrieve a piece of trash.

For years, any time I could spare a few days from my private consulting work to do a little prospecting for myself, I'd head down east and look for my Holy Grail: granite. To actually find some left me breathless. I remembered how excited I had been, splashing up and down the creek looking for more outcrops. Though I only found a few and they were extremely weathered, the strike and dip of the planes in the granite were unmistakable, all with the same orientation. Each time I took a reading on my Brunton compass I got goose bumps, confirming each outcrop to be just like the others, all trending in a northeast/southwest direction. I was giddy as a schoolgirl.

But that was then, this was now. Back to business. I tied a marker of plastic yellow flagging tape to a small sapling, pulled a black indelible marker from my pocket and wrote "core #1" on the tape. The proximity to water, needed to cool the drill bit as it grinds through rock and flushes debris from the cased hole, made this a perfect location for the first of many core samples I hoped to take. Meanwhile, Tulip, tired of aggravating the squirrels, trotted up and sat at my feet. I bent down on one knee to give her a hug.

At that moment, above me, right on a line of where my head had just been, the tree trunk exploded in a shower of bark and splinters. Now maybe it was because I watched lots of Westerns as a child, but I knew the whine of a ricocheting bullet when I heard it. And, just like in the Westerns, I instinctively dove toward the creek bank for cover, yelling, "Stop! Stop! Don't shoot!"

I scrambled under some undergrowth, frantically looking for Tulip.

She was in front of me, splashing through the shallow water at a dead run. Like all good hunting dogs, she was racing ahead upon hearing a gun fire to finish off or tree her master's quarry. Then the rifle cracked again. With an agonized yelping noise, Tulip collapsed and lay very still.

I stared, paralyzed with shock and fear, at the underside of her body. Blood was seeping from somewhere near her shoulders and slowly turning her mostly white belly a bright red. I wanted to go to her but was afraid to raise my head. One of her feet twitched. She raised her head and struggled to rise but was unable to. She just looked at me pathetically, then fell back.

"Easy, girl," I said, stretching out my arm

to her. "Stay. Stay there. I'm coming. Just hold on, girl." I lay still about a minute longer before calling out again.

No one answered.

I heard no movement. Nothing except the trickle of the creek and birdsong. I pushed up on my shaking knees and crawled to Tulip. She was still breathing. Carefully, I lifted her limp body, scrambled up the slippery bank, and slogged my way back through the dense undergrowth to the open pasture, then ran for the Jeep. Jeans wet from the knees down and soggy boots made me feel like I had exercise weights on my ankles.

I gently laid Tulip on her side in the cargo area, dug out a T-shirt from my overnight bag and tied it around her chest. I realized the front of my shirt and jeans were soaked with bloody water. It had even spattered on my boots. My hand shook as I pushed Tulip's lip over her teeth to expose pale gums. I mashed a spot with my index finger; very little color returned. She'd lost so much blood. I slammed the cargo door shut, jumped behind wheel, and gunned it for a veterinary hospital I'd passed a couple of times on my way into town.

An agonizing hour after the veterinarian and

her assistants took Tulip from me and disappeared into surgery, the waiting room door opened. The vet, a nice young woman with a pretty smile and hugely pregnant belly, walked over quietly and slipped into a chair beside me.

She patted my knee.

My heart squeezed.

"Don't worry," she said, "She's going to be just fine. I know it looked bad, but it's just a flesh wound. She did lose right much blood, but you got her to us quick so she didn't go into shock. We're sewing her up now and giving her some blood, some antibiotics. With a little rest, she'll be good as new."

I felt tears pool and looked away.

"Wounded hunting dogs are my specialty," said the sweet vet, thankfully ignoring my emotional state. "We get a lot of them around here."

"Really?" I sniffed.

"Yeah. Not so much this time of the year though," she added pensively. "It isn't deer season. Probably someone poaching."

Taking a deep breath of relief, I said, "Thanks so much for helping Tulip without her even being one of your patients. I'm sure you saved her life."

"Now, not a bit of that, sug," she said,

waving her hand dismissively. "We're just glad you got her here in time. Didn't I hear you tell my assistant you're working nearby?"

I rose to leave and said, "Doing consulting work," my pat answer that basically says nothing and usually stops further questions. "I'm staying at the Morning Glory Inn. I gave my cell number to your assistant. Give me a call if you need me."

"Okay, sug, you go get yourself cleaned up," the young vet said, struggling to heave herself to her feet. I gave her a hand. "And don't worry," she added. "She's had plenty of painkillers and she'll rest easy here."

It was almost six o'clock when I left Tulip in the vet's capable hands. Deciding I'd had about all the fun I could stand for one day, I headed for the Morning Glory. A little painkiller for myself sounded like a capital idea.

I dug out a pint of excellent Kentucky whiskey, Jack Daniel's, black label, from my overnight bag. I always carry one in case the need arises and, by my way of thinking, a hitchhiking rattlesnake and a dog who took a bullet were need enough. But the mini refrigerator humming away in the corner had no freezer, and thus no ice. So I picked up the ice bucket to head for the ice machine that lived on the far end of the second-story porch running along the full length of the old mansion turned inn.

I pulled the door open, and there was my tall, beautiful daughter, her fist raised ready to knock.

"Yikes!" she said.

"Yikes back at ya," I said. "What're you doing here?"

"Dad told me about the rattlesnake, so I thought I'd come down to see for myself that you're okay."

"I'm fine," I said and shoved the bucket into her hand. "Go get some ice."

She was back in a flash. I plopped a few cubes in two tumblers, poured a generous splash of Jack Black in each and handed her one. Then I collapsed with mine in one of two overstuffed chairs.

"So tell me what happened with the snake," she said, plopping down in the other.

I told her about the rattler and also about Tulip's "hunting" mishap and all the other little events of the day that kept nagging at me and threatening to become big ones. Like not finding Gladys or talking to her for weeks.

Henri — she's been called that since a few

minutes after she was named Henrietta Gail twenty-three years ago — sucked on her ice, studied her glass, then got up to add fresh cubes and another splash of Jack.

I wrinkled my brow. "You know how I feel about more than one drink without food, especially if you're planning on driving."

"Not to worry," Henri said. "I'm going to stay here with you tonight. Let's order Chinese and get drunk."

"Fine by me." But I knew she wasn't here out of concern for my emotional state or for idle chitchat. She had another reason for being here, likely her usual reason. I waited her out. We drank, ordered, plied our chopsticks, and talked about her business. She's a talented photographer when she's not being a student.

Finally, on her third glass, Henri revealed her primary mission. "You know," she said, "Dad was so happy he was able to do something for you today. You should do something nice for him in return."

A twinge of guilt pricked me. I'd told Bud I would cook him dinner tonight. However, it was a very small twinge, considering how many times I'd cooked for him only to hear, "Oh, I forgot to tell you, babe, I have a meeting," as he dashed out the door.

I twirled the ice in my glass with my

41

finger, sighed noisily and said, "Henri, I'm not interested in excerpts from *Henri Cooper's Complete Guide to Etiquette for Divorced Parents.* Your dad and I get along perfectly fine the way we are. When are you going to stop trying to turn back the clock?"

"I'm not trying to do any such thing," she said huffily. "And besides, you said it yourself, you get along fine. So why can't we just be together as a family?"

"Because you and your brother don't even live at home anymore, for one thing, and because I really don't want to do thirty to life at the Women's Correctional Institute in Raleigh, which is exactly what would happen if I tried to live full-time with your father again. You and your brother have got to give up this fantasy."

"But . . ."

"No *buts.* I'm not going to discuss it another second."

"Okay." She took another sip of her drink and moved on to her second-favorite topic: her love life. How the latest *amour de jour* just wasn't working out, how she planned to extricate herself from the relationship and still remain friends, yadda yadda yadda.

Around midnight I pulled two old oversized T-shirts from my bag, threw one to Henri and headed to the bathroom to change. I don't remember ever actually owning any pajamas. When I came out, Henri was sprawled on her side of the king bed snoring softly. I slipped under the covers on my side, turned out the light, and smiled at the promise of teasing her with the snoring thing later.

FOUR

The next morning, a Tuesday, I was up and dressed at seven-thirty in my summer "uniform" for field work, which consisted of a form-fitting, short-sleeve T-shirt and skinny, straight-leg designer jeans. Designer jeans because the denim is soft, stretchy, and lightweight when compared to old-style jeans. Form-fitting garments because they are vital in the constant battle to keep ticks and other creepy crawling critters from finding their way under your clothes. And, if they do, they are mashed against your skin so it makes it easier to detect them when they move. Fitting my laces into the eyelets of my field boots and executing a quick double knot, I was ready to go hunt down Gladys.

I left the still-sleeping Henri a note and took off for the Five-Eight Café, which besides being located on Highway 58 and operating from five a.m. to eight p.m., serves a mean bowl of grits and some stand-up coffee. I knew Henri would want me to have breakfast with her at the Morning Glory before she returned to Raleigh, but I wanted some space.

I sat down at a gray metallic-flaked Formica table — not just reminiscent of the fifties but actually from the fifties — ordered coffee, and started going over my field notes.

The waitress hadn't even come by when I heard a familiar voice behind me.

"I can't believe it. Twice in two days?"

Nash Finley. A warm rush washed over me, dropped straight to my lap, and snuggled in. "I could say the same thing," I said.

"The Belgrade foreman wasn't at the quarry yesterday. Had to go back today. Aren't you going to invite me to sit, Cleo?"

I motioned to the chair across from me.

Nash pulled out the chrome and red plastic chair. I stared at him, realized I was fanning myself with the menu, and set it aside.

He pulled a cigarette from his T-shirt pocket.

I wrinkled my nose.

He put the pack back and said, "If I didn't know better, I'd think you were prospecting."

"Yeah, but because you used to be a geologist, you know better. No proposed roads so no need for finding rock to crush up and put into asphalt, right?"

A bright-eyed young waitress in a white uniform with a fake camellia pinned to her ample bust appeared, bent across our table, swiped it with a greasy wet cloth, and said, "Ya'll having the early bird — two scrambled eggs, grits, and bacon?"

"That's good for me," I said and looked at Nash.

Nash nodded at the waitress and she bustled off. "Well, just because there aren't any proposed roads down this way for the next twenty years doesn't mean you haven't heard insider information from one of Bud's cronies at the DOT," he said and flashed one of his sparkling smiles. Damn, he was pretty. "I'm just curious, that's all. And I miss the shop talk you and I used to have when we worked together." His right hand lay next to mine on the table. He extended his index finger, crooked it over my wrist and rubbed it gently.

I slowly withdrew my hand, but shook my head and smiled in spite of myself. Usually I'd be miffed at someone underestimating me so blatantly, but Nash was a curious mix of lovable, harmless good guy and dark,

46

mysterious sex object. Besides, talking shop was definitely not what I was interested in doing with him anymore, but the cautious side of me still had questions.

"Okay, Nash. So at the risk of sounding like someone from one of those reality dating shows, why didn't you call me when you moved to Raleigh?"

"In the first place, I can't imagine you watching a reality dating show, and in the second place . . . well, we weren't getting anywhere, were we? I mean, what was I supposed to think? I'd tried all my best moves. Just couldn't get you in the sack," he said with a big grin.

I gave him my best horrified look and quickly scanned the nearby tables to see if anyone had overheard.

He tilted his head like a curious dog and said, "Have you looked in the mirror lately? A woman who looks like you . . . I figured I just wasn't doing it for you. Figured you were waiting for . . . whatever it is you women wait for."

I tried to think of a witty remark, but my voice was trapped somewhere. Thankfully the waitress delivered our orders and as we dug into our food, I had the feeling he was as grateful as I for some time to think.

We finished eating and I was tucking my

napkin under the heavy crockery plate when Nash said, "Maybe we could start over. Be friends this time."

"Let me give that some thought," I interrupted. "Right now, I've got places to go and people to see."

Friends? Not likely. Something else? Maybe.

Before going to Gladys's house, I needed to get rid of the mud and broomstraw on the side of the Jeep, so I pulled into the local car wash. I'd deal with the scratches and dents when I got back to Raleigh. While I waited, I flipped open my cell to call the vet and check on Tulip. A perky receptionist pronounced Tulip patched up and ready to go home anytime. I said to let her rest another day, that I'd pick her up on the way back to Raleigh.

An attendant brought the Jeep around — washing had definitely improved its appearance — and I eagerly jumped in to check off number one on my list of important things to do today: talk to Gladys about what to expect when the drill crew arrived.

As I approached Gladys's house a little shiver ran down my spine. I certainly didn't want another run-in with her darling kiddies. Anxiety turned into disappointment though as I bumped down the dirt road and her house came into view. There were no cars in the driveway or parking area.

She still wasn't home.

I considered driving back into town and looking for her car, then decided that, for the next few hours at least, my time could best be spent finishing my grid. If she wasn't home by lunch, I'd go looking for her then.

At the site, I hesitated before getting out of the car. Should I strap on my 380 Beretta or my baby nine? I decided against it. After all, yesterday had undoubtedly been just a hunting accident. I wasn't about to shoot at someone just for being stupid. And the rattler? Well, I guess it's feasible that the varmint crawled in the Jeep several days ago when I was airing it out after Tulip had horked up a half-digested squirrel on the seat.

The morning went by quickly. I marked the location of drill holes and core samples with flags and tape like a woman possessed. I was flagging the second half of the 150-acre field of relatively clean Coastal Bermuda hay that had just received its first cutting of the summer. Since Gladys still had this part of her land under cultivation, she'd wanted me to synch my testing with her hay baling.

By noon, sweat was plastering my ponytail to the back of my neck so I wiggled my finger down to the bottom of my jeans pocket and fished out a piece of essential field equipment: a rubber band, one of those clear ones that won't tangle in your hair. I wadded my hair into a ball and made a few quick loops of the band around it. I tried to fan a little of the humid air under my damp T-shirt, but it did little to cool me and the rumble in my stomach was turning into a full-blown protest. Time for lunch.

Making my way back to the Jeep, I stopped at an old well beside a tenant house that had seen better days. The presence of water made this another perfect location for taking a core sample.

I pulled a roll of bright yellow surveyor's tape and a marker from my back pocket, tied a long strand of it to an old four-by-four corner post that held up what was left of a rickety tin roof and numbered it. Then, because it is impossible to stand next to a well and not look into it, I leaned my elbows on the wide stone rim to gaze down at the water below. I wondered how far it was to the surface. Looked like about twenty feet. When I was getting ready to spit and refine my calculation, I noticed a shape in the far shadows.

Something rather large and black was down there.

I moved to the other side of the well and squinted into the shadow, using my hands to block out the sunlight. But I still couldn't make heads or tails of what I was seeing. A nylon rope, presumably attached to a bucket, hung from an overhead crank down into the water. I reached for it. My intention was to pull it to the object and see if I could get a sense of it by touching it with the rope.

I'm five-nine, but the width of reinforcing cinder block around the old stone well made it so I couldn't quite reach the rope. Straining, I pushed myself out over the well wall and reached for the rope again.

You know how it is when you're about to do something stupid but can't stop yourself, so you do it anyway? Well, that's how this was. One minute I was stretched to the max, reaching for the rope with one hand, the other on the wall, and the next minute my feet seemed to lift off the ground and I was dropping like a rock to the water. Fortunately, I'd rolled in the air so I smacked the surface flat on my back.

I came up sputtering. "Goddamnit!" I yelled and punched the water with my fist. "You idiot!" Cursing a few more times, I grabbed the rope, willing myself to calm down and assess the situation.

That's when I realized two things. One, there was definitely a bucket at the end of the rope. It was submerged about three feet below me. In fact, I was standing on it — it was what was keeping my shoulders and arms out of the water. And two, the large black object reeked. I mean it seriously stunk. I'd smelled deer carcasses in the woods and this was similar, only way worse.

I reached over and gingerly touched the object. A shiver shot through my body that wasn't caused by the chilly water. The object was wrapped in heavy-gauge black plastic. White plastic clothesline held the bundle closed, and closer inspection revealed a loop caught on a sharp stone in the wall, thus keeping the stinking object from sinking.

I probed the bundle a little harder and heard a soft popping sound as several large gas bubbles erupted from underneath it, creating even more of a stench. One bubble was so vile my eyes burned and I retched up what was left of my breakfast grits. No doubt about it, whatever was inside the bundle was well past dead, and I did not want to be anywhere near it.

With Olympic strength I never knew I possessed, and using the nylon rope twisted around one leg as a boost, I shimmied up the well like a monkey with his tail on fire. They say hard work is its own reward so maybe I've got years of working outdoors to thank for the strength to pull myself hand-over-hand up the rope. I don't know, but my high school gym teacher would have been proud. When I reached the top of the well, I swung my free leg over the rim, grabbed a corner post, pulled myself to the edge and collapsed in a soggy heap on the solid ground.

I lay there until my heart stopped trying to hammer through my rib cage and my breathing returned to normal, then sat up and wrapped my arms around my knees. I wanted to cry, not only for my bad luck in finding what I was pretty sure was a body in the well, but because I had a sinking feeling I knew whose body it was.

I trekked back to the Jeep, retrieved my cell from my purse, and dialed 911.

FIVE

There was now no way to keep my site a secret until I completed my testing. In a little over an hour, the flag-strewn field was swarming with deputies, detectives, and an assortment of crime scene investigators from the Onslow County Sheriff's Department. It was indeed a human body in the well. I had answered the sheriff's repetitious questions as to why I was on the property and how I came to fall into the well. Now I was getting time off for good behavior.

Or so I hoped. But it didn't last long, because Sheriff Sonny Evans soon reappeared by my side.

"Ma'am," he said, fanning himself with his hat, his face red from the heat, "we're fixin' to load up the body now but before we go, I'm wondering, how much longer will you be on Miz Walton's property?"

"As long as it takes for me to complete my tests. Even if it turns out to be Gladys

— um, Miz Walton — in the body bag, it won't stop me from testing or exercising my option if I choose to do so. My contract is with her *or* her heirs," I said.

Sheriff Evans shifted his weight. He was a beefy man, in his late fifties I'd guess. "And you think her kids would want you to keep on testing . . . that is, if it is her . . . ?"

I squirmed a little. "Why wouldn't they? My contract would pay them way more money than they'd get if they developed the land."

"So you're saying her heirs would get this option money you told me about?"

"That's correct. And royalty money." Seeing where his thoughts were headed, I added, "Of course, we don't even know who it is yet."

"No. But this being her land and all, it simply offers food for thought that them lazy kids of hers would get all that money if she was gone. You did say you haven't seen or spoken with Miz Walton in over two weeks, right?"

Well, well, I thought. *Robert Earle and Shirley seem to have a reputation in the county.* "That's right, Sheriff. I've been away on another consulting job. I've tried to call her but with no luck. As soon as I got back to this job yesterday, I went by and she still wasn't home. Her car wasn't there this morning either."

The sheriff nodded, then said thoughtfully, "Even though the body looks to be pretty decomposed, a lot of things could affect that, being wrapped in a plastic tarp, being in water. We'll just have to wait for the medical examiner over in Chapel Hill to tell us who this poor soul is and when they died. It may take some time."

We both paused to consider the implications.

"In the meantime, we'll start a search for Miz Walton. And I'll have a talk with Robert Earle and Shirley. Let them know what we found up here."

"Well, if you don't need me any longer . . ." I ducked back into the Jeep, opened the glove compartment, pulled out my business cards, and gave him one.

"Please let me know the minute you find out who that is," I said, nodding in the direction of the ambulance as it bumped out of the pasture and onto the dirt road.

"I sure will." He studied me in something resembling admiration. "You know? You're one strong lady to be able to pull yourself out of that well."

Replacing his hat, he tipped it courteously and hurried back to the crime scene.

■ ■ ■ ■

I was ready to pack it in. I left a message on Henri's voicemail telling her I was headed home. I try to always let her know where I am. Before returning to the Morning Glory to pack up, however, and since, owing to the July heat, my clothes were now almost dry, I made a quick swing by Irene's house.

Her Honda was still in the drive. The hummingbird feeder was now completely dried out. Even the line of ants that had been mining the feeder for dried sugar crystals had given up and left. It was probably a waste of time to knock on the door, but I did so anyway. No answer.

Still engaged in wishful thinking, I walked around to the back of the house. Maybe Irene had a garden or a tomato patch, and I'd find her there. Sure enough, I found a garden, but no Irene. Just bees, bugs, and lots of weeds.

Since I was here anyway, I figured I might as well jiggle the back door for the second time in as many days. I climbed the cinderblock steps, crossed the porch and tapped halfheartedly on the door. Silence. The door was still locked.

I looked around the yard. A floor freezer,

a small wooden table and chairs, an old wooden lingerie rack, a charcoal grill. Nothing out of the ordinary.

I went back to the Jeep and sat there for a few minutes. Then, because I just couldn't stop myself from committing a federal offense, I got out and walked over to Irene's mailbox. Well, maybe it would be okay just to look inside the box, as long as I wasn't shuffling through stuff or taking anything.

Quite a bit of mail was crammed in the box. It certainly looked like more than a few days' worth. Near the bottom of the pile I found a postcard. It was from Gladys's sister in Venice, Florida. That made her Irene's cousin.

It read, "Having a ball. Wish you were here. Sister." I put the card back in the pile and the pile back in the box. I felt totally frustrated. Time to retrieve my hound and go home.

At three thirty I picked up a much improved but still weak Tulip, carefully loaded her in the Jeep and we were on our way. Since it was Tuesday, not Sunday, I didn't have to fight returning beach traffic and was home by six.

First order of business: ditch the field boots and nasty clothes and slide into my idea of a lounge set, namely, a tank top and drawstring workout shorts. Second, toss some spaghetti sauce in the microwave to thaw, pour a glass of nice Chianti, and look through my mail.

That got me to thinking about the postcard I'd seen in Irene's mailbox.

Over the past year I'd had many conversations with Gladys, often with Irene present. Whenever Gladys talked of using the money from the sale of her land to move into a retirement community near her sister in Venice, she always included Irene. But it always seemed to me that Irene was noncommittal about the prospect.

The microwave beeped to remind me to stir the container of sauce. Just as I did, I heard a car door close. I padded across the old heart pine floors, moving from the back of my remodeled 1940s bungalow to the front. On tiptoes at the door, I peeked through one of the arched windows of glue chip glass.

Damn. How did Bud know I was home?

Henri, of course.

I opened the front door before he could ring the bell. Whipping flowers from behind his back, he inquired, "Dinner ready?"

Ignoring the flowers, I turned on my heel and said, "Almost." Back in the kitchen, I started making a salad with whatever produce was left in the crisper drawer.

Bud followed me and found a vase for the bouquet. After poking noisily around in the fridge, he found what he was looking for, a lonely bottle of Bud Light way in the back.

After slugging a gulp, he topped off my Chianti for me.

"How's Tulip? Henri told me what happened. You're lucky you didn't get your head blown off."

"She's fine," I said. "She's outside. I'll call her in, in a little while." I paused, stirring the sauce again. "Turns out yesterday's events pale in comparison to what happened to me today."

I had to admit it, I was glad to have someone to talk to about finding the body in the well. Not an everyday occurrence, and I was pretty sure the full impact hadn't hit me yet.

"I'm all ears," Bud said.

I didn't get very far into relaying the weird events of my day before Bud grabbed the paring knife from my hand and took over slicing the cucumbers and heirloom tomatoes. Maybe he was worried I was getting overexcited as I told my tale.

As we ate, I finally put voice to the suspicion that had been nagging me since I'd found myself at the bottom of the well.

"You know, I think someone might have snuck up on me, lifted my feet out from under me. Made me flip over and fall into the well."

Wiping his mouth with his napkin, he tucked it under the edge of his plate. "Now, Cleo . . ." He paused, as if to gather his thoughts enough so he wouldn't come right out and call me crazy. "Why would anyone want to kill you?"

"Not kill me. Just scare me away, keep me from testing the property."

"Scare you away? Keep you from testing? Who? Why?"

I shrugged. "Maybe someone doesn't want the land sold. Maybe they don't like the idea of me 'raping' the land with a quarrying operation. Maybe someone doesn't want a quarry next door or in the same town or even in the same county. Or maybe someone thinks a quarry nearby will lower the water table and dry up their well. Et cetera, et cetera."

People get all kinds of crazy misconceptions from misinformation, but I can tell you this: I've spent the majority of my career as a geologist working for large mining concerns and no one immediately falls in love with the idea of a quarry or an oil well or anything else of that nature being in their Zip Code. Never mind that those things make the lives they lead possible. It's the NIMBY philosophy: Not In My Back Yard.

"Cleo, I thought you said no one knew about this project, that you were keeping it top secret. Who would know about your plans?"

"Well, people close to Gladys might know. Her children, of course, and her cousin, Irene — who's also her housekeeper. Which is another thing, Bud. I can't find Irene either."

"Maybe she's with Gladys. But let's get back to her kids. You'd think they'd welcome the idea of their mom working a deal with you if it meant big bucks. Then, after she's gone, they'd inherit a larger estate, right?"

"Right. That's what I'm worried about. I mean, what if that's Gladys's body? Wouldn't the kids be the most likely suspects . . . the ones with the most to gain?"

"Okay, okay. I realize a body in a well's a serious thing, but it could be anyone — a migrant worker, a hobo. Don't let your imagination turn this into a made-for-TV movie. Thinking Gladys's children might do her harm, or you, for that matter, is . . . well, it's just too much of a stretch. It makes way more sense that they'd be thrilled you were going to make them some money."

"Well, they sure don't act like it," I muttered, remembering Robert Earle's threat to pitch me off the porch.

"Are you going to put off your testing until you find Gladys or until you learn the identity of the body?"

"No. In fact, I'm going to move up my start-up date to Monday if I can. Those boys at Statewide Testing do a lot of work for me. They're pretty amenable to conforming to my schedule."

"You'll see," Bud said. "The sheriff will find Gladys, probably with her sister —"

"Cousin," I corrected.

"Whatever," he said. "Tell me again what you're prospecting for. What you've told me so far is fascinating."

Oh, please. Fascinating. He was toying with me and I knew why. Never mind that I still kind of wanted to be toyed with by Bud. He was tall, in great physical shape, handsome in his own way and, without a doubt, the best I ever had. Thing was, there was a whole world full of men out there I hadn't had. One in particular came to mind. Besides, I knew where a relationship with Bud would lead and I didn't want to go there again. Been there, done that. I checked my watch and said, "Don't worry about helping me with the dishes. I'll take care of them. You run along, I know you're busy and I have lots to do myself."

"What? No dessert?" Bud said as he plopped down on the couch beside Tulip, who looked up at me and gave several sheepish thumps of her tail. She knew she was breaking the rules. So did Bud. Difference was Tulip was a dumb animal. My ex, on the other hand, well . . .

I pulled him up and said, "No, sir. No dessert. It's Tuesday night in Raleigh. Aren't they having two-for-one drinks at one of your favorite watering holes?"

"Probably. But I'd rather be right here with you . . . having something sweet." Bud took a step toward me and traitorous bits of my body flamed.

Knowing I couldn't trust myself another minute in the same room, I gently steered him toward the front door and said, "Good night, Bud. And consider yourself paid back for the successful snake extraction. You certainly have a way with reptiles."

Six

It was after three o'clock Wednesday afternoon before I'd caught up with my paperwork on other jobs and had time to call Statewide Engineering and Testing, the firm I'd hired to test Gladys's property. Just as I hoped, they were able to move my job up and start on Monday. Then, because I'd tossed and turned all night reliving the past two days and going over what I'd learned, what I didn't, what I understood, and so on, I looked up the number for the Onslow County Sheriff's Department. Waiting to be connected, I searched my tired brain for his name, beyond "Sheriff." I'd given him my card, but he hadn't given me his.

I got lucky when a deep voice said, "Sheriff Evans."

"Hi, this is Cleo Cooper. I'm the geologist who, er, found the body yesterday."

"Yes, Miz Cooper. What can I do for you?"

"First, I was wondering if you've been able

to get in touch with Miss Walton yet, and second, I thought of something I'd like to pass along to you. I don't know if it will be of any help, but I'd feel better if I shared it."

"Good. I can use all the help I can get. As to Miz Walton . . . no, I wasn't able to speak to her yesterday. I did talk to her son and daughter this morning. Woke them up . . . at nine o'clock." I detected disdain in his voice. "They say they don't know where she is. According to them, she's been gone about two weeks. They don't seem concerned. Said she does this sort of thing often."

"Huh," I said. "Well, I've known her a little over a year, and during that time, she's never just taken off. Anyway, I think she'd say something to me if she was leaving town. She knew I was getting ready to start testing."

"Seems logical."

"What did her kids say about me finding a body on their property?"

He chuckled. "They sure don't think much of you. They seemed shocked about the body, but neither one acted like they thought it could be their mother."

"Did you know that Gladys Walton has a

housekeeper? Her cousin . . . Irene Mizzell."

"No, I didn't. You're the first person to
mention her."

"Well, she's the other reason I called, to
tell you about her. She lives in one of the
tenant houses on the farm — down the first
path on the left after you pass Gladys's
driveway — and I wasn't able to find her
while I was in town either."

"Huh," he said. "That's kinda hopeful. I
mean, could be they're off together somewhere. I'll check that out right away, Miz
Cooper, 'preciate your call."

After I hung up, I called my lawyer to ask
if I could take her to lunch and run a few
questions by her. She said she and Penny,
her paralegal, were dieting but that I could
meet them in the backyard of her house
where they planned to split a grapefruit and
get a little sun. I took that to mean they
were also taking off early. They probably
worked late last night. I told her I'd see her
there.

I had hired Sharon Peele for my divorce.
She was one of a rare, (indeed, near-extinct)
species of lawyers: a non-greedy one. Afterward, both she and Penny turned into good
friends, even though, unlike me, they were
young, single, and constantly on the prowl.

As I headed over to join them an hour later, I stopped at Jersey Mike's and snagged a sub-to-go for lunch. On the way to my lunch date, I mulled over once again the timetable and details of what had happened since Gladys Walton had disappeared off the radar.

"Wow. You've had some amazing things happen to you while prospecting, but a dead body in a well, jeez, that's a first," Sharon said, when I finished my tale.

"Yeah. Good times," I said dryly. I wasn't sure if they had paid as close attention as they might have. Penny's eyes were wide. Was it the story or my roast beef sub?

"I know we've got a strong document," I said, "but what if the body does turn out to be Gladys? Could I run into any problems? Up till now, all I've invested is my time, but once I start testing, I'll be sinking a ton of money into this project."

"You're right to be considering all contingencies," Sharon said. "But I suggest you carry on with your plans until you actually do hit a snag because so far nothing's really changed. Even if the body does turn out to be the landowner, you're covered. Someone could try to stop you with an injunction, but since you have an ironclad option to test as part of an ironclad lease agreement prepared by the best in the business, *moi,* we'd probably come out on top of any legal challenge."

Probably?

"And," Sharon added, "soon as you finish testing and exercise your option, I've got your Memorandum of Lease all ready to be filed in the Onslow County Courthouse."

I nodded, rubbing my finger across my bottom lip.

"Stop frowning," Sharon said. "It causes wrinkles. Just keep moving ahead. Everything will be fine and if it's not, you have a good lawyer."

Easy for you to say, I couldn't help but think. This little venture could cost as much as three million dollars, not to mention a million dollars to exercise the option once the discovery was confirmed. My plan was to acquire a term loan and secure an operating line of credit. The note and deed of trust would be in my name and even though my banker was a long-time friend who believed in me, the bank he worked for was a very conservative one, the kind that requires proof you can repay what you borrow. Therefore the need for additional cash to cover the initial testing that would prove the deposit existed. That would come from my personal retirement account, the entire half million of it.

A small piece of consulting work concerning a fault underlying a proposed industrial site in the Triassic Basin near the town of Merry Oaks kept me busy through the week and into the weekend, but Monday morning I was back at Gladys's farm.

Heavy gray clouds scudded overhead as I held the gate to the field open and waved the drill crew through. Two tattered Ford pickups, the drill foreman in the first and a crew member in the second, rumbled through. They were followed by a gargantuan drill rig. A soaking overnight rain had made the ground soft. While a good thing for drilling, it was bad for supporting a 25,000-pound drill rig, so I was a bit on edge.

The guys who make up a drill crew are known as doodlebugs, and nicknames are usually the rule. Jimmy Ray Boswell was called Mule, for example, and Pete Willis was Stick, short for Dipstick.

Since Pete was the crew member charged with on-the-road maintenance of the vehicles, I could understand his moniker, but Mule . . . Either Jimmy Ray was real stubborn or let me just say it, the nickname often made him the subject of some prurient thoughts during long, hot workdays. Though neither of them could expect a casting call from a Hollywood agent looking for a pretty face, both could pass as plausible body models. More important to me, each was a well-seasoned professional.

I'd really lucked out in the experience department with Statewide's foreman for this job, Lewis Winkler. Wink had been drilling holes all over the world for nearly forty years. But unlike his crew, he actually showed the wear and tear from those four decades. He had a lazy eye and skin like a leather jacket someone had left near a radiator too long.

"Hey Wink," I said, shaking his hand.

"Ready to go?" He said, unfolding his field map and orienting it to the acres of little orange flags stretching out before us.

"Yup," I said. "I paced 'em as far apart as I could since you guys charge like you're using solid-gold drill bits."

He chuckled. "Well, you'll have to take that up with the big wheels at the home office. I'm just a little cog." He turned to the crew and made like a boss. "What are you two knuckleheads doing? Why ain't you drilling?"

They grinned at him.

71

"Mr. Boswell. Mr. Willis," I said, nodding at each one in turn.

"Miss Cleo," they replied practically in unison.

"Where you want us to start, Wink?" Mule asked.

"How about hole number one? That make sense?" He pointed to the southwest corner.

"Yessir," Mule said, at which signal he and Stick politely tipped their hard hats toward me. Wink folded his field map and got in his pickup to follow them. I brought up the rear, my heart in my throat.

Simply put, at about thirty dollars a foot for every hole I drilled, depending on the depth to the top of the rock and the number of holes we got in every day, I figured to be going about thirty-five grand a day in order to prove the existence of the vast granite deposit I was sure lay under my feet. And these were just the holes to see how deep the rock lay; we would still have to come back and take core samples to be sure what *kind* of rock it was.

I visualized my underground granite mountain as somewhat like Pilot Mountain, North Carolina, only smaller and still covered by millions of years of accumulated dirt, or overburden. Pilot Mountain is an enormous dome of metamorphic quartzite that covers over thirty-five hundred acres. By my estimations, the granite mountain below Gladys's farm would cover about four hundred acres and extend below ground every bit as far as Pilot Mountain was high: twenty-four hundred feet. That, boys and girls, is a lot of rock.

A similar structure was being mined in Fountain, North Carolina, but that's about fifty miles back to the west. Up until now, it was the easternmost occurrence of crystalline rock past the fall line — that boundary between the foothills, where water drops abruptly enough to create a fall, and the coastal plain — on the East Coast. But that granite had been exposed in a flat expanse covering about three acres. Easy to see.

In fact, that granite had been part of the recorded geologic history of the state since the 1930s. My rock, on the other hand, wasn't well exposed anywhere. I was relying on pie-in-the-sky evidence: a few crumbling, weathered boulders I'd found in a creek and differences in vegetation I'd noticed when comparing aerial photos pulled from the Onslow County GIS office with the woods as they actually existed on Gladys's farm. From a rented plane, I was able to see that although the farm had been allowed to reseed naturally after being clear-cut, the trees were stunted in a large elliptical area covering about three hundred acres in the middle. The surrounding woods were denser and the trees themselves larger and more robust.

Since I often worked with timber cruisers while consulting, I'd learned that during the first twenty-five years of growth, trees rooted in shallow soil on top of granite grow slower than trees with hundreds of feet of soil below them. The field I planned to drill lay at the southwest edge of where I hoped my granite mountain came close to the surface of the earth.

Therefore, the granite — if it existed — would lie somewhat deeper here. I felt the panic rising and reminded myself of the basics I already knew.

Mule and Stick set about leveling the rig with four enormous hydraulic pads that dropped down from the undercarriage. After the bit dropped through the sandy soil like a straw through a Wendy's shake, Stick started handing Mule the corkscrew auger flights, which were pinned together, one after another, to push the bit deeper and deeper into the ground, until it hit something too hard to drill through.

We zipped through the first thirty feet.

Sweat had already begun to bead on my upper lip, and it wasn't from my hard hat holding in heat. Forty feet. Forty-five, and the bit made a few little chirps. At fifty-eight feet, it made a screeching noise as the bit's teeth ground into an impenetrable layer. The flights bucked, vibrating the drill apparatus that towered above us.

"Top of the rock!" Mule shouted to me over the throbbing of the big diesel engine. I gave him a thumbs up and watched as he flipped the reverse switch to bring the flights above ground. Dirt spiraled off them, creating what looked like a huge ant hill around the hole. As each flight came up, the crew stopped, knocked out the auger pin, unhooked the flight, then placed it back on the rig.

"Maybe it'll get better," Wink muttered to me. He marked the depth to the top of rock on his field map in red ink.

I nodded and said, "*Better* is a relative word. It all depends on what kind of rock you're looking for." For example, removing fifty-eight feet of overburden isn't cost-effective if you're mining a band of limestone thirty feet thick. If, however, after fifty-eight feet you hit hard, valuable rock hundreds of feet thick, then it becomes profitable.

Wink looked at me curiously. "We're looking for limestone, aren't we? The Castle Hayne Formation?"

I didn't want to show my hand yet. Might as well just wait and let the evidence speak for itself after the first core — if there was to be one.

I moved away from the rig and Wink followed. "I'll be in the woods, flagging," I told him. "Meet you guys at twelve and we'll go into town for lunch."

"Okay. See you then," Wink said and headed back to the rig. The crew was still stacking the auger flights in preparation to move on to drill hole number two.

I drove across the field, pulled out of the gate, and turned left, as if pulled by some magnetic force. At the old house by the well I gave an involuntary shudder at the sight of all the yellow crime scene tape, and not just in memory of what I'd found in the well.

The tape presented two problems: one involved the length of time the area would be cordoned off — we'd need access to the water in the well when we started drilling core samples; second, I didn't know why the house had been marked out of bounds too. I got out of the Jeep for a look-see. At the tree where the tape was wrapped and tied in a knot, I noticed a gap of about twenty feet before it started again. I looked at the end of the tape, which was dangling there. Obviously, the cops had run out and simply not bothered to close the gap.

To me, it resembled a welcoming entrance. Who'd know if I just walked around a little? After all, I was the one who discovered the crime scene in the first place.

I quickly covered the distance to the old house and stepped onto the sagging porch. I had to duck to pass through the front door. People must have been shorter back then. Once inside, it was apparent the place still served a useful purpose. Each room was filled with freshly cut bales of Coastal Bermuda hay — it gave off a rich, comforting aroma that reminded me of childhood summers and the hum of my dad's lawn mower.

Dim light filtered through cracks in the walls. No insulation, no sheetrock. Life was tough in the good old days. Back out on the porch some squeaking under it — mice I guessed — made me look down. At my feet was a large black ashy spot circled with white chalk. Luckily, I hadn't stepped on it. Maybe it meant something to someone at the Sheriff's Department. And someone had snubbed out several cigarettes here, though there were no butts.

I squatted and sniffed but didn't detect the odor of ordinary cigarettes. Instead, the aroma was more pungent, like a cigarillo or a Swisher Sweet. Leaning over the porch edge, I saw that ashes had fallen through the cracks and . . . *Well, well, what have we here?*

I carefully picked up a tiny scrap of brown paper and sat back on my heels. Someone had definitely stood at the corner of the porch and smoked a cigarillo. Then came a revelation: This was the perfect place to watch the well and remain unseen.

Had someone been watching me? *Get a grip,* I scolded myself. *You've got a big job to do.* Brushing the ashes from my fingers, I left the creepy rundown shack and headed back to flag drill holes in the woods.

SEVEN

After about four hours of hacking my way through stubbornly resistant underbrush, I sheathed my machete and made a quick check for ticks. Back on the road where I'd parked, I opened the Jeep's cargo door and felt a pang of loneliness for Tulip.

Though she'd miraculously not been seriously hurt in the hunting mishap, she needed at least a week to heal before returning to her hard-charging life as my field buddy. Henri had agreed to keep her at her house until I got home Friday. I sure did miss that hound.

Funny how just knowing you're responsible for the safety of someone else made you feel safer too. Worked for me anyway.

As I slugged down a bottle of spring water, I heard a truck approaching. Turning, I saw Robert Earle Walton's black Escalade slowly bumping over the cut hay field. Nice ride. Expensive too.

Gladys had told me that both kids had received modest trust funds when their father died, which kicked in when they turned twenty-one. She'd explained the funds as both a curse and a blessing. The blessing being that Robert Earle and Shirley could never get at the principle; the curse, that the income was just enough so that neither of them had ever tried to stay gainfully employed for very long. They knew they had enough to get by.

I leaned against the back of the Jeep, my arms crossed. Trying to appear even more nonchalant, I propped one boot behind me on the back bumper.

Robert Earle hopped out of the SUV. "Hi! How are you today, Miz Cooper?" he said, all bright-eyed and bushy-tailed. What was wrong with this picture?

"Huh. Fine, Robert Earle. How're things with you?"

"Doing just fine too. How's that testing going?"

"Not much to say yet. Just got started. Have you heard from your mother?"

"Say, I brought some soft drinks for you and your crew. Think they'd want one? Got 'em all iced down 'n everything."

So now he was concerned about my hydration? I said, "I take that to mean you still haven't heard from her. What about Sheriff Evans? Has he updated you about whose body that was in your well?"

"No, he hasn't been back in touch . . . Pretty awful, huh? Why, people in town can't talk of another thing." He sounded as if he was trying out for the part of the gossipy old maid in a community theater play. He retrieved a Styrofoam cooler from his backseat and carried it to my Jeep.

"Well, thanks, Robert Earle. I'm sure the crew'll appreciate all those cold drinks." I looked up at the parting clouds and patches of blue in the sky. "Especially now that the sun's coming out."

"Glad to do it," Robert Earle said as he hefted the cooler into the cargo area.

"What about your cousin Irene? Is she back yet?"

Robert Earle's jolly mask momentarily slipped as anger flamed in his eyes, but he blinked it away in an instant. He reminded me of a cuttlefish I'd seen on the Discovery Channel, flashing different colors with each change of emotions.

"Those two," he said with a fake little laugh. "I swear, they've got everybody worked up over nothing. They'll be back when they're good and ready. You'll see."

"So you're saying you think your mother

and Irene are together?"

"Sure. Besides, Mom's done this before and it only makes sense that Irene's with her. Where else would she be?"

Good question. "I don't understand. Gladys has done this before? When and for how long?"

Again the flame followed by the fake smile and phony chuckle. "Oh, she's been doing this on and off for years now. Shirley and I worry sick about her at times, but we've learned to live with it. Besides, as Mom gets older, we have to think of her well-being."

"What does that mean? Her well-being?"

"You know. Keeping her safe, of course."

"I see." I looked at my watch. My crew would be wanting to go to lunch and I wanted to ditch this clown. Plus, I was anxious to see the drilling report about how far down the guys had drilled before reaching rock at the other flags. "Thanks for the sodas. I'm meeting the crew for lunch and I'll see they get them then."

"Let me know how those test results look," he called after me as I drove away.

Right, Robert Earle. And you let me know the very moment they find Elvis.

The crew followed me down Belgrade Swansboro Road to Highway 24, also known as Freedom Way because it leads to Camp Lejeune Marine base. We pulled in at Minnie's Luncheonette at the edge of the greater Jacksonville area. Over a meal of chicken and pastry, baby limas, and cornbread, we discussed the results from the two dozen holes Statewide had drilled while I was being entertained by the delightful Robert Earle.

Turns out they were much the same as hole number one, all fitting the visual image I had of my granite mountain. I was pleased with Wink, Mule, and Stick and told them so. Just as the waitress brought our banana pudding, included with today's special, I excused myself from the table. On my way to the ladies' room, I thought I glimpsed a familiar face. Stepping into a hallway that led to the restrooms, I casually glanced back. Sure enough, it was the other half of the Walton brood.

The rabbity-looking guy with her was familiar too, I just couldn't place him, though I was sure I'd seen him fairly recently. The prominent nose, small mouth, and top teeth sticking out. By the time I'd washed my hands, I'd made an executive decision. I was going to stop by Shirley's table and see if she was feeling as friendly as her brother this morning.

"Hi, Shirley," I said. "How are you today?"

"Well, I'll be darned. So nice to see you," Shirley fawned. "Robert Earle said he'd been over to your testing site and you and your crew were working like a bunch of ants. Just drilling and drilling."

Imagine that. Drill crews, just drilling and drilling. I bit back the sarcastic comment. "They're busy, that's for sure," I said and looked at her friend. He had a tattoo on the bottom side of his forearm — a pair of angel wings sprouting from a small plane. Now I remembered — he was the pilot who'd flown me over Gladys's farm.

Similar thoughts were obviously forming themselves in his mind. He snapped his fingers. "Cleo. Cleo Cooper, right?"

"Right," I said. "You've got a good memory. Better than mine, I'm afraid."

"Oh, for goodness sake," Shirley said. "Where are my manners? This is Ivan Thorpe . . . my boyfriend." She scrunched up her plain face — which didn't help it one bit — and grinned at Ivan. He returned her gaze and they clasped hands, mooning at each other across the table.

Suppressing an involuntary gag reflex, I smiled and said, "It's nice to see you again." Then, turning to Shirley, I added, "When I talked to Robert Earle this morning, he said

84

you guys aren't too worried about your mom . . . He says she does this kind of thing all the time?"

"That's right. She'll be back when she's ready."

"What about Irene?"

"Oh, I'm sure they're together. In fact, Ivan saw them not long before Mom left."

I looked at him.

"Yeah, right," he said. "I saw them in the Red and White over on Second Street. I believe it was around noon."

"When was that?"

"I can't remember exactly. Heck, it could've been the day they left. Might've been getting road snacks. You know, come to think of it, I believe it must have been Monday, because I went in there to pick up bottled water right before I flew out to pick up clients in Greensboro."

"Monday, like last Monday?"

"No. The Monday before that."

"So, two weeks ago?"

He shrugged. "I guess that's about right." Jiggling Shirley's hand, he said, "We need to go now, sugar, if we're going to have time to go by the jewelry story before I head back to the airport."

Shirley blushed. I could tell she was bursting with pride. She looked up and said,

"Ivan and I are getting engaged."

Just then I noticed my crew was headed for the cashier, so I gave the lucky couple my very sincere best wishes and left.

On the sidewalk in front of the diner, I said, "Wink, you know, I'd just as soon keep all our test results confidential. Very confidential."

"You're the one paying for the information. That means you're the only one privy to the results."

"Just so we're all on the same page. You might need to remind Mule and Stick to keep it buttoned too."

"Gotcha," he said, in a way I felt I could trust.

EIGHT

Friday arrived and a whole week of testing was drawing to an uneventful close — uneventful only in the sense that I hadn't found any bodies, been threatened or shot at, or encountered a dangerous wild animal. It was, however, certainly true that my granite mountain was taking shape, and that was all the *eventful* I wanted. Connecting the dots of data on my field map, I could almost see that mountain, and I could hardly wait until I had all the data. Then, when fed into a computer program, it would create a three-dimensional image that anyone could marvel at.

Fortunately for me, my son, William, a year older than Henri, was handling that part of my project. We'd already set a tentative date, based on when I thought I'd have enough data, for him to come up for a visit and show me the images. I would do it myself except I've discovered that spending prolonged periods of time on a computer stir feelings in me of violence, mayhem, and murder. Better to let Will do it. Besides, the kid was fresh out of school.

At twenty-four, he'd already received his masters in marketing and economics from the Calloway School of Business at Wake Forest University last year, and he'd started his own search engine optimization company. Despite the fact that he would forget more about computers before lunch than I could hope to know in two lifetimes, starting a business was tough to do even in normal times. In a recession, it was damn near impossible. I had no doubt his massive intellect and boyish charm would take him to the top of his game, but giving him a leg up and helping myself at the same time . . . no-brainer.

This last morning of our first week of testing looked to be a red-letter day for me. We'd moved out of the field Tuesday afternoon and been in the woods for the past three days. Wink had brought in a bulldozer to push trails for the rig and we'd finally cut our way to the creek, where there was sufficient water to take our first core sample of the rock underneath all that dirt.

As I trekked along the raw trail the crew had made — mangled underbrush, small, downed trees — my thoughts went again to Gladys. Yes, I was a little worried but I also missed her. She'd been so excited about "our project" as she called it. I wished I'd taken more time with her when we were together, but I had always been in a rush to get somewhere or do something. Stopping briefly to bend a willowy limb off the trail, I wondered why it is that humans never seem to learn to appreciate the people in their lives until they're gone.

I, for one, never appreciated my own mother until I lost her at the tender age of nineteen, during college and right before I got married. One day she was there, seemingly healthy and vibrant, and the next she'd departed the planet by way of a heart attack. That was more than twenty-five years ago.

The trail broke into a Y-intersection, and I stopped and listened. The sound of clanging metal told me the crew was replacing the standard drilling bit, the one we used to drill through overburden, with the rotary core bit. Tungsten steel inserts or industrial diamonds make it possible for a rotary bit to cut a circle through solid rock.

Continuing on my way, my thoughts went back to my mom. If I'd known I'd be privy to her marvelous wit and wisdom for only such a short time, I would have paid more attention. Maybe that's why I was so bummed by the disappearance of Gladys Walton, who was about the age my mother would be now.

From the first minute I'd met her, most everything about Gladys reminded me of Mom. I'd looked forward so much to being able to share with her the test results. Remembering some of our conversations, I wondered now if what I took for excitement at the possibility of receiving such a large sum of money was, in reality, relief at finding a way out of a bad situation. Maybe the farm and taking care of two grown children — ones who had the money but not the motivation to take care of themselves — had gotten to be too much for her. Maybe she saw the sale of the land as a way to exit gracefully. To, in effect, kick the kiddos out of the nest by selling said nest to me.

Rounding a curve, I saw Wink's pickup. Then a roar like a monster outboard motor filled the air. Mule had started the pump that would pull water from the creek to cool the rotary coring bit as it ground through the granite, creating a cylinder of rock about two inches in diameter and pushing it up into a five-foot long hollow pipe, the core barrel. The thrill of discovery made me lose my boss-lady cool and I ran the rest of the way to the site.

Wink handed me a hard hat and said, "Did you see that guy . . . Robert Earle? He was looking for you."

"No. Must have just missed him," I said, failing to mention that this morning I'd hidden my Jeep in the woods for the express purpose of avoiding another of his friendly visits — his fourth this week. I had no intention of encouraging him.

"So what'd he want?" I asked.

"The usual. Just wanted to know how things were going and where you might be. I didn't tell him anything."

"I'm not worried about him, though he is turning into a pest. He'll get the information he's supposed to when I'm ready."

I pulled my field map from my backpack and rolled it out. Mule threw the rig in gear. The sweet crunching, screeching sound of the bit taking its first bite of hard rock was music to my ears. Wink smiled, seeing my big grin, then motioned me toward the front of the rig. He dove into the cab and retrieved some topographic and aerial maps. He flattened them on the door, holding them in place with magnets.

"We'll need to cross the creek when we finish on this side," he said, pointing to it

91

on the map. Gladys's property was fairly evenly divided, east and west, by the creek where I had first seen the granite outcrops.

"I've checked out the bridge," I said, tapping its location on the aerial and penciling it in on my own map, "and I'm sure it will take the weight of the rig. But I'd feel better if you checked it out too."

"Already did, it's in good shape. Probably put in by the loggers who cleared this place, what — twenty-five years ago?"

"Something like that."

"Well, the concrete drainage pipes are still strong, there's no sign of cracks, and it's plenty wide for the rig. I did use the bulldozer to push a little extra dirt around the side where we gotta make our turn and a little extra on the far side. Held up the dozer just fine."

"Let's go check it out again while they finish cutting this section of core, just to be sure," I said.

We had finished our inspection of the farm bridge and were heading back to the rig when we heard a shout from Mule. We hotfooted it back and when we reached the rig saw Stick bending over the first box of core. His eyes were the size of saucers. He stood up, wiping his muddy hands on his jeans, and pointed to the box. "Gawd almighty, I ain't no scientist, but I believe this here's 'sposed to be impossible."

Mule, positioning the bit to drop it back down the well and cut another core, yelled over the deafening clamor of diesel and gasoline engines, "I told him that could be some kinda limestone we ain't never seen! Just 'cause it looks like granite and it's hard as a wedding dick, don't mean it is . . . does it?"

"Yes, Mule!" I yelled back at him. "It does!"

"Holy crap. You got to be kidding," Wink said, picking up a few small chips of the rock that had fallen to the ground. He clicked them together and cocked his head. "Girl, do you know what this is gonna be worth?"

I laughed. "I might be blond, Wink, but I can assure you, I know what it's worth. Again, just make sure you guys keep clammed up about this until I'm ready to make it public."

As the five-foot sections of granite came up, Stick removed them from the core barrel, broke them into smaller sections and fit them into wooden crates. After I logged in the first section, I used my rock hammer to knock off a lime-sized hand sample from a section of core. I got out the small, folding magnifying glass I kept on my keychain and inspected the rock.

"Hello, sweetheart," I said. "So glad to finally make your acquaintance." Medium-grained granite gneiss. I turned it in my fingers. "You and I'll get to know one another real good later on —"

I was interrupted by the change in pitch of the rig's engine. Mule was adjusting the hydraulic controls, increasing and decreasing the pressure on the bit, which had begun to make screeching noises.

"Sonuvabitch!" said Mule. "It's so hard it's already dulling the bit!" I sighed, well aware it would be the first of many diamond-tipped bits. But what the heck, I was going to be rolling in dough soon, right?

About the time we finally got the first hundred feet of core in the crates, Mule threw the rig's diesel engine into neutral and said, "Ain't anybody around here hungry but me?"

I checked my watch and frowned. "It's only noon." I didn't want to quit. "Want to cut a few more sections?" Mutinous stares from the crew. "Okay, okay," I said. "Pull that tarp over the crates. We'll leave the truck here. I don't want it parked on the street in town. We'll take Mule's truck to lunch. I'm buying."

On the hike out of the woods, the guys were full of questions about how I'd known to look for granite in this spot. "I don't understand how it got here. You mean it's just in this one location?" Stick said.

"Picture the rocks on the West Coast. How they stick up from the beach, the waves pounding them. Well, this rock used to be like that. This is a small mountain of the same type of rock that makes up the basement of the East Coast, the rock that lies hundreds of feet below us. The fact that it's so hard that it chewed up our very expensive coring bit is why it's still here. All the other rock around it eventually eroded away and left this little mountain, kind of like Pilot Mountain, or Stone Mountain in Georgia. When we start to quarry it, we'll expose places that will show us where the waves beat away at it."

"For real?" asked an incredulous Stick.

"Yup," I said as we got to the field.

Wink, walking with Mule ahead of Stick and me, looked back at us and said, "Wonder what he wants."

I shielded my eyes from the burning sun and saw the figure coming toward us. It was Sheriff Evans.

NINE

"Ma'am," he said, tipping the brim of his hat.

"Sheriff," I said and swallowed hard, trying to delay the inevitable, "this is my foreman, Mr. Winkler. My drill crew" — I indicated the guys.

"Fellers," the sheriff said.

"What brings you out today?" I said, feeling my guts twist.

The sheriff fiddled with his hat and looked down.

I sensed he would be more comfortable passing the news to as few people as possible, so I said to the crew, "I'll catch up with you guys in town."

Sheriff Evans looked me square in the eyes and said, "M.E. in Chapel Hill has identified the body you found."

Oh no. It was her. My mouth went dry. "Okay."

"It wasn't Miz Walton."

My knees stopped buckling. "God, what a relief. But who was it?"

"Well, remember you told me about the other lady, her cousin" — the sheriff paused to pull a small spiral notepad from his shirt pocket — "a Miz Irene Mizzell?"

"Yes, yes . . . ?"

"It was her. Detectives believe the cover that was wrapped around her was off a charcoal grill, but we'll let them and crime scene people determine that for sure."

"How'd they make the identification? I mean, she and Gladys were both about the same age, kinda looked similar, you know . . . Same build, same silvery-gray hair, cut in similar styles . . ."

The sheriff stopped my babbling: "Dental records. They don't lie. It really helped that both women went to the same dentist in town. Had for years."

I started not to ask, then decided it would be best to know all the details available to me. "How did she die?"

Sheriff Evans looked down, flipped his hat again and said, "Bullet to the back of the head. The hole looks to be made by a bullet from a small-caliber gun, we don't know the exact caliber yet. We'll know that when forensics is done. Of course we weren't expecting it to be accidental, not with her wrapped up and dumped down a well."

"No. I guess not." I had to look down at my field boots. I was not going to act all girly and cry. No way.

"Detectives and crime scene guys'll probably have some more questions for you."

"That's fine. Anything I can do, of course. But what about Gladys?"

"We have a Silver Alert out on her. But remember, this isn't our only case. If you're thinking a small town like ours never has murders, think again. This time of year we just about triple our population with migrant workers. Some summers we get as many as three killings. This year, we've already gotten two, and it's not even halfway through the season yet."

"I had no idea."

"Well, just letting you know, so you don't expect us to wrap this case up like one of them episodes of *Law & Order* and end up disappointed."

"I'll keep that in mind, Sheriff, and thanks for coming all the way out here. I appreciate it."

In spite of the sad news of Irene Mizzell's murder, lunch was a celebratory affair. After all, we were in the process of making a historic strike. One that would not only make a pant load of money for me and generations of my heirs but would lift the economy of the surrounding small towns. Considering how hard the great recession had hit eastern North Carolina, that would be a very welcome thing.

"You two pecker heads need to brush up on your rock identification," laughed Wink, as two waitresses sat down bowls of cole slaw and field peas, a platter of fried catfish, and a basket of hush puppies.

"I knew what it was," Mule said. "I just try not to make Stick look dumber than the rocks we drill."

Stick tipped his chair on its back legs and said, "Hey, I was pretty sure it was . . ."

I interrupted him, looking up at the waitresses, "Know what? I think you're all smarter than a room full of Harvard lawyers. Matter of fact, I know you are. Now, dig in. We've got work to do."

As the waitresses hurried to the next table, Wink looked at the boys, scowled, and pulled an imaginary zipper across his lips. They nodded and switched to a weightier topic: Wrestlemania. I listened to their funny banter, elated on the one hand that my site was proving to be all I had hoped for and deeply troubled on the other that the body of a murdered woman had been found there.

Wink later dropped me off at my Jeep so I could snag a bottled water and some field notes. I decided it wouldn't hurt to walk off some of the calories from the fried lunch, so I told the guys I'd walk the rest of the way. When I got to the site, all three men were wearing funny expressions.

"What's up?" I asked.

"Somebody tampered with one of the boxes," Stick blurted, pointing at the granite core samples in the back of Wink's truck.

"What?!"

"Whoever did it was in a hurry and cracked the top of one of the boxes. There's a sample missing."

"Damnit to hell!" I stomped away about ten paces, hands on my hips, my back to the crew. I was just too angry to speak.

"I'm sorry," Wink said. "I should've done more than just nail those crates shut. I should've put metal bands around each one of them."

"Ya think?" I snapped and was instantly sorry. I held my palms out like a crossing guard, closed my big mouth, and retreated into the woods. I found a perfect time-out stump and sat myself down. *What the hell is going on?* I thought I knew, but I took the time to ponder the events of the last few days and listen to the birds. How I missed Tulip with her wise brown eyes. When I was sure I was calm and the crew had had sufficient time to think about what they'd done, I went back.

As I stepped back into the clearing Wink said, "I swear, I just didn't think anyone would go to the trouble to traipse all the way back in these woods and find the crates."

"Yes," I said. "You should have, but we were all pretty excited. Just be more careful next time. Anyway, I've got this property tied up tight enough, so whoever did this . . . well, they went to a lot of trouble for nothing. Besides, I've been thinking — it's obvious who did it."

"Who?" asked all three men practically in unison.

"That numb-nuts, Robert Earle. He's got access. And he's proven himself to be a grade-A horse's ass. Just because he's been acting like Little Mary Sunshine lately doesn't fool me for a second. It sucks, but no harm done.

"Now let's see if we can get the rest of our first core in the box before we break for the weekend. Come Monday, we'll finish our overburden drilling on the east side of the property, cross that creek, and see what our mountain looks like on the other side."

Late that afternoon, I waved at them as they drove off, then pulled the gate closed and padlocked it. I was pocketing my key when I saw Robert Earle's Escalade heading my way. *Damn.* And I was so close to leaving. Well, at least he was being friendly these days. I decided to keep it that way by playing dumb about the sample and conveying my condolences on the death of his cousin. Still, the thought of him creeping about in the woods, spying on the crew and me made my blood boil.

He got out and walked toward me, a legal-size manila envelope in his hand.

"What's this?" I asked as he handed it to me.

"Something that says you don't need to come back here anymore. You're done. I'll be taking over the testing of my mom's property from now on."

I set my poker face to cool and collected. Then, on second thought, dialed it up to cocky and said, "Number one: I have a legal contract signed by your mother. We've discussed this before, Robert Earle. And number two: I asked you already, what is this?" I held up the manila envelope.

"Open it and see for yourself."

I didn't move my eyes from him until I'd slipped the document from the envelope, then glanced down at it. It was an option to test signed by Robert Earle and Shirley, and signed by their mother designating them as her agents. I noticed the date too: it had been signed a month ago, five months after my document.

But instead of it being a legal document between an individual doing business as a private consultant and the landowners, like my option, a company name was listed as being the party of the first part, or the one to exercise the option.

I'd never heard of the company — I.T.N.F. TestCo Group — but a quick scan of the pages revealed it was Charlotte-based. I checked inside the manila envelope as if I were looking for something else. I turned it upside down, shook it, and looked inside again.

"Where's your Power of Attorney?" I asked. "Gladys would have told me if any such document existed."

"I couldn't lay my hands right on it when I left to come find you, but I'll have it in your hands tomorrow."

I stared into his eyes. He blinked then looked down and to the right. *Amateur.*

I dialed my poker face to smart-alecky

smirk, tossed the envelope and document on top of his size-12 Pumas, and said, "I'll be back with my crew bright and early Monday morning. Don't impede them or my testing in any way or you'll find yourself facing a lawsuit, Robert Earle. A big one."

He bent and retrieved his option as I got in my Jeep and hit the down button on my window. Then I dropped the smirk and said, "Don't fuck with me, Robert Earle. 'Cause, trust me, you won't like it."

By the time I reached the highway back to town, I realized the reason my teeth were aching was because I was clenching them so hard. I wrapped my fingers around my jaw and massaged until the throbbing subsided. As I did, I noticed my gas gauge indicated I was near empty. I was so furious I had to actually think about it for a minute before deciding a fill-up might be in order. Since the Jeep's tank was just about empty, I turned right onto Belgrade Swansboro Road rather than heading into Stella.

Within a few miles, my outward appearance was probably pretty normal. Inside my head, however, I was still jumping up and down and screaming. *That dumb fucker! Who does he think he's talking to? Power of Attorney? I'd bet my bottom dollar he didn't have one. And what or who in the hell is I.T.N.F. TestCo Group?*

I.T.? International Testing? Or maybe — The ring of my cell interrupted my furious thoughts: Henri. Well, I didn't have the time nor was I in the frame of mind to speak with her. I saw the Exxon station I was looking for and pulled up to the pump.

The gas gurgled and foamed as it flowed into the tank. Grackles and cow birds strutted about on the concrete looking for something to eat and all the while information collided in my mind.

Gladys wasn't dead. The test site was proving to be all that I'd hoped for. The Walton siblings were trying to take over my life's work. Well, only a little over a year of it, but still, it was what I'd wanted all my life.

Power of Attorney? Is that what that "Mom disappears like this all the time" crap was about? Were they trying to have her declared incompetent? If so, how long had that smarmy scheme been going on? Had it caused the uneasiness I sensed in Gladys sometimes? Did she suspect her children wanted her out of the picture?

It made sense. In the way that two adult children being so lazy and conniving as to try to take their inheritance before their mother was dead ever makes sense.

And another thing: like the old cliche says, there are no coincidences. Robert Earle and Shirley's cousin was dead. Bullet-to-the-back-of-the-head dead. And cousin Irene looked a lot like Gladys — same height, weight — and from behind . . .

I shuddered so violently that the nozzle jerked out of the tank and gas splashed down the Jeep's side. I blinked and shook my head. "No," I said out loud, then looked around to see if anyone heard me. *No, it can't be.* It was almost impossible to bring myself to contemplate such a thing, her own children trying to kill her? No. I simply wasn't going there. Better to ask the following question: if Gladys wasn't dead, where was she?

I sloshed some black, greasy water on the spill with the windshield squeegee and bent to wipe it dry with a paper towel. Then I slowly stood up.

I knew where Gladys was.

TEN

I sat on the edge of my bed at the Morning Glory Inn, booted up my laptop, and looked up the white pages for Venice, Florida, the town where the postcard in Irene's mailbox originated. Also the town where Gladys's sister lived.

Gladys always called her "Sister," but her real name was Penelope and, according to Gladys, she'd never married. That meant her last name would be Gladys's maiden name, Bulla. How many Bullas could there be in Venice? Three, I discovered easily when I found the name. Two were men. One was listed P. Bulla. Bingo!

I grabbed my cell and in a flash her number was ringing in my ear.

There was the sound of the phone being picked up, after which, a frail voice hesitantly said, "Hello?"

"Sister!" I exclaimed as if I'd had known her all my life. "Hi. It's Cleo Cooper. You remember, Gladys's friend from Raleigh? I know you guys are having a grand time and I hate like the dickens to bother you, but could I speak to Gladys for a moment?"

"Oh. Sure. She's right here . . ." She cleared her throat and called out, "Gladys! It's for you, dear."

I heard a muffled "Who is it?" followed by some shuffling about with the receiver. Then I heard Sister say, "I can't remember who she said she was, but it's not the kids."

Gladys's voice came on the line. "Hello?" she said hesitantly.

"Gladys," I said, almost tearful with joy, "it's me, Cleo. I've been worried sick about you. You didn't tell me you were going to see your sister. Are you all right?"

It seemed like relief I heard in her voice when she said, "Oh Cleo, I'm so glad it's you. I didn't mean to worry you, honey. I . . . I've been meaning to call, but Sister and I have been so busy. And, well, I just needed to get away for a while. Besides, I thought we'd covered everything about your testing. I can't wait to hear how that's going. It is going well, isn't it?"

"It's all going fine, Gladys. It's Robert Earle and Shirley I'm having a small problem with."

"Oh?"

"Gladys . . ." I said, realizing I didn't know where to start. "Um, Gladys, have you ever signed a Power of Attorney, a document giving your children authority over your affairs?"

"Oh no. They aren't trying to pull that stuff on you, are they?"

"Actually, they are. More important, do they know you're at Sister's?"

"No. They called a couple of times, but she convinced them I wasn't here. We haven't talked about this Cleo, but sometimes, I just feel the need to get away from my children. I'm sure you can understand. You don't need to worry about that Power of Attorney thing either. They might try to make me think I'm crazy and they might be trying to make others think I'm crazy, but I'm not. I'd never sign anything they wanted me to. If I had, I'd have been out on my keister a long time ago."

"Good grief, Gladys! Why would your children try to do that to you?" I asked though I was pretty sure I already knew the answer.

"Oh they're not bad kids. Just hard-headed is all. And a little spoiled."

You think?

"Sometimes, if they don't get their way, they try to take over. But I just let it pass. It always does. That's why I'm down here."

"They've done this before?"

"Well, there was the one time when they wanted to grow houses on the land instead of hay. You know, back during the development boom in the nineties? But I was having none of it. Made 'em real mad, but I'm not scared of them because —"

"Gladys," I interrupted, "I hate to say this, but maybe you should be. A little scared of them, I mean. At least until I get the testing finished, get your option money to you and the rest of the legal papers filed to see that you're paid for the land, according to our agreement, over the next ten years.

"You see, Gladys, there's a complicated set of hoops we both need to jump through to complete this transaction in a bomb-proof manner so that no one can ever have you declared anything but what you are — a kind, loving, and very competent person."

I paused, getting my breath. "Until then, I'd really feel better if you laid low somewhere. Not at Sister's anymore either. Since it's crossed their minds that you could be with Sister, it would only take driving down there to find you. Then you and Sister would have to deal with an unpleasant situation with no one to help you. You need to have me or an attorney with you when you see them."

"I understand what you're saying, but I'm not scared of —"

"I know you're not scared of your own children. I'm not saying that . . ." I paused again, not knowing a nice way to say what needed to be said. The elephant in the room, as it were. I just dove into it: "Gladys, I'm afraid I have some bad news for you. It's about Irene."

"Irene. I've been calling her for days. I knew it — she ran off with that scumbag crab fisherman from Manteo, didn't she? Married him too, I bet. I knew it. I just knew it."

She yelled for Sister, then came back on the line and said, "When she wouldn't say for sure if she was going to live with Sister and me, I knew something was up. That woman is bound to live a life of drudgery despite all I can do for her —"

"Gladys," I said softly.

"What? She didn't marry him? She just ran off with him? How do you know?"

"Gladys . . . Irene is dead."

"Dead? He killed her?"

"No, he didn't kill her. At least, I don't think he did. I don't know who —"

"Where is she now?" Gladys interrupted

"Still in Chapel Hill at the Medical Exam-

111

iner's. It takes a long time to do all the testing required in a homicide."

"Homicide?" she said in a tiny voice.

"Please listen to me. You need to be up here where I can talk to you and you can see to Irene's . . . funeral details. I'll explain the whole thing when I see you."

Even as I was talking, I pulled up American Airlines on my laptop and booked a flight for Gladys arriving at eleven fifty, Saturday afternoon. I gave her explicit instructions on how to get her E-ticket at the airport and where I'd pick her up.

Exhausted, emotions tossing about in my head like clothes in a dryer, I hung up and flopped back on the bed. My cell clanged. I looked at the screen and saw Nash Finley's name. Hello, distraction.

"Yes," I said.

"Hello, there. Where are you?"

"Where do you want me to be?"

"Always the mysterious one. Actually, I remember you saying how much you love Wrightsville Beach and was hoping you were coming down, it being Friday and all."

"I might be. Why?" I said, wondering just exactly what I was doing.

" 'Cause I'm down here at the Blockade Runner. I had to be at the Castle Hayne quarry today so I decided to spend the night. What would you say to a little dinner at the Bridgetender? A couple of really dry martinis, some prime rib, and . . ."

"And?"

Okay, now I knew what I was doing.

"And whatever you want, sweet pea, for as long as you want."

"Well, the dinner sounds good, anyway. What time?"

"Say, seven-thirty?"

I checked my watch. Though it would take a little over an hour to get there, I could make it, easy. Mickey Mouse screamed from the watchface, "Don't do it!"

"I'll meet you at the Bridgetender."

Hey, it was just dinner and right now I needed some cheering up. I figured I could always get my own room at the Blockade Runner, right? So, being always prepared — you never know when one of several clients I have in the area might call and want to discuss a job over dinner — I pulled my three-inch, peep-toe sling-backs and black body-hugging tank dress made from that material you can wad up for a week without wrinkles from my bag and got ready for dinner out.

The Bridgetender Restaurant, overlooking the Bridgetender Marina and the Wrightsville Beach drawbridge, is one of my favorite restaurants, not only because they serve delicious food, but because it is so relaxing to sit and watch the comings and goings of boats. I could do it for hours, but relaxing wasn't what I had in mind when I got there at seven forty-five on the dot. Better to have Nash one martini ahead of me in situations like this.

He was sitting in the bar area in the front of the restaurant and stood and motioned to the bartender as I sauntered in. He looked me square in the eye. In heels, I almost reached his six-feet.

"I've thought about you several times since I saw you last week," Nash said. "Thought it might be fun to see you again, but now . . ."

"But now?"

"But now, I'm kinda scared." He grinned.

You and me both. "Poor baby. You have nothing to fear from me as long as you play by the rules."

"Well, by all means. What are the rules?"

"No shop talk."

The bartender handed me a very dry Grey Goose martini with three olives. Just the way I like it. Nash clinked my glass with his and said, "Fine by me."

ELEVEN

Is there anything better in the whole world than waking to the sound of waves pounding and seagulls crying and your whole body's limp as a noodle from having used every muscle — and I mean *every* muscle — all night? The answer to that is no — unless you've never experienced it. In that case, you probably can't imagine how I ended up in a dark hotel room feeling not the least bit guilty. Sex with Bud had always been great. As long as we were married, I never strayed. In all those years — and a few times since — our sex life never lost its fire. But always, always, it had a tender component. A sweetness, no matter how frisky we got.

With Nash, on the other hand, there was definitely no sweet component. In all honesty, it even had a scary edge, which made me wonder if I'd ever go to bed with him again. Then certain memories brought on a jolt like I expect a cattle prod would produce, and I knew I would.

But, hey, I did check into my own room. I should get points for that, right? I felt around in the bed. No Nash. A vague memory of pushing him out of the bed sometime before dawn came to me. I guessed it was before dawn. Heavy blackout drapes made the room dark as a pit so I couldn't really tell. I looked over at the nightstand for the digital. It wasn't there. Must have been the crash I heard in the wee hours of the morning. I felt something scrunched up under the cover at my feet and dug around between the foot of the bed and the sheets. My dress. Further exploration rendered one shoe and, finally, my watch. I held up the glow-in-the-dark Mickey with big numbers and saw that it was nearly seven o'clock.

Dang, I was burning daylight. Gladys would land in Raleigh and be waiting for me by noon, besides which I knew Nash expected me to have a leisurely Saturday morning breakfast with him. I planned to be long gone by then.

I got up and went to McDonald's feeling just fine about leaving Nash without so much as a good-bye. The morning after first-time sex, so awkward. Truth be told, he'd probably appreciate my giving him some space. Besides, I had a big project going and while it might be a workless weekend for him, it definitely wasn't for me. Halfway through my McDonald's iced coffee, I concluded I was going to survive last night's debauchery. Without taking my eyes from the road, I dug my cell from my purse — a maneuver I was becoming remarkably brilliant at — and said, "William," the voice command to dial my son.

He answered immediately. "Hey," he said.

"Hey, Will," I said, "how's my firstborn?"

I could hear the smile in his voice. "Fine. What're you doing?"

"Actually, besides wondering how you are and wishing I could be in Miami with you right now, I was hoping you could do me a huge favor."

"You know you can visit me anytime you like, and I'm always more than happy to help you if I can."

What a good boy I raised. "Great," I said. "What I need is one of your excellent computer searches on a company."

"What's the name?"

"I.T.N.F. TestCo Group. The C in TestCo is capitalized. I believe they may be a Charlotte-based company. I know if anyone can find out who they are, it's you."

"Okay. Give me the rest of the day. By the way, I've got everything set up for the computer presentation for your banker. All we need now is data."

"I'm on it," I said, amused at the implication, however politely packaged, that I should get on the stick and start feeding data to him as soon as possible and not leave everything to the last minute.

"I've got a lot going on here with my stuff too. But I'll call you soon as I have something."

"Thanks, honey. You're still coming up to Raleigh Thursday, aren't you?"

"Absolutely, but I'll talk to you before then."

It was almost eleven when I pulled into the driveway of my house in Raleigh. Tulip was so excited to see me I was afraid she'd explode.

Henri was behind her. "She's really missed you," she said. "And I have too. What's on your schedule? Are you going to have time for me today?"

"I've got a friend coming in at the airport around twelve. If you could pick her up, I'd be eternally grateful."

"Grateful enough to loan me your Bakers with the stacked wooden heels?"

I grabbed my overnight and my garment bag from the seat and headed inside. "Seriously, what I really need is the time to go over the core logs from that consulting job I finished last month out in Wyoming, and write up my report. I was supposed to have sent it in last week . . . And yes, you can borrow my Bakers . . . once." I might be a practical dresser on the job, but for all other occasions, I love clothes.

"Okay then. I'll do airport duty. I must say, though," my daughter said primly as she followed me through the door, "I really expected you home yesterday afternoon to take care of your paperwork. What were you doing all day?"

"I had some, uh, catchup work I needed to attend to. I took care of it." *Well, how else would you describe it?*

"What kind of . . ."

"Better scoot, sweetie, if you're gonna make it to the airport in time," I said as I ushered her back out the front door. "I'll phone my friend and let her know how to find you."

As soon as she left, I called my lawyer.

"Sharon, I believe I've got a problem."

"Shoot."

"First of all, Gladys isn't missing anymore. She's been in Florida with her sister this whole time, hiding from her kids. Turns out they're trying to have her declared incompetent. They claim they've got a Power of Attorney. Say they're going to take over the test site with a new option they've gotten with some company I never heard of."

"Oh. Is that all?" Sharon said nonchalantly.

"Should I be worried?"

"Is there a P.O.A. filed anywhere?"

"Gladys says no."

"Then you're okay. My advice would be to keep Gladys away from her kids until we get this thing wrapped up legally. That way she's protected and so are you. I take it from what you've told me that she may need protecting from her kids."

"That looks to be the situation to me."

"Okay, then. Carry on. But just to be on the safe side, might be best if you have Gladys inform that sheriff guy of her whereabouts. You said he had a Silver Alert out on her. He'll probably want to talk to her in person too. You can arrange that easily enough. Also, her children should be informed that she is safe. Maybe she knows a good time to call when they aren't likely to be home so she can just leave a message. Something to the effect that she's visiting a friend . . . that would be sufficient."

■ ■ ■ ■

Shortly before one o'clock Henri delivered a distraught Gladys to my door. I ushered her into my kitchen, poured her a cup of coffee and did my best to tell her all I knew about what had happened to Irene. I wanted to spare her the grisly details, but she kept asking questions, and isn't knowing the truth the quickest path to recovery from losing a loved one? I think it is, so I did my best to tell her everything.

"I just don't understand," Gladys sniffed, dabbing her eyes. "Irene wouldn't hurt a fly. Everyone loved her. She was a pillar of the church"

"What about her gentleman friend? You implied you don't like him very much," I said.

"Oh, I only complained about him because I thought Irene was too old to marry again. But he's a nice man, a good man. And I believe he loves Irene . . . or loved her."

"When was the last time you actually saw her?"

"Right before I left for Sister's. It was a Monday and she'd come over to my house to help me put up strawberry preserves. She and I went to the store. I needed some more lids." Gladys got a faraway look in her eye. "Oh, I almost forgot, we dropped my car at Buster's garage, up on the main road. You know, to check it out for my trip. While Buster worked on it, we went back to ladle and seal. Then she drove me back to Buster's to pick up the car, and I said good-bye and reminded her to go back the next day while the kids were out to dinner to put the jars on my pantry shelf. She said she would."

"Why the next day and why when the kids were out?"

"I can tell you don't know anything about canning. I guess I'll have to teach you." She patted me on the hand. "Preserves can't be moved for twenty-four hours after they go into the jars. Has to do with the seals. And why when the kids were out? Well, Irene liked to avoid them because they always ask her to do extra stuff for them."

"So how long were you at home before you left?"

"All morning. We dropped the car off early and worked through lunch. Then, after she left me at Buster's, I got on the road. When I go to Sister's, I always stop just over the Georgia line in Brunswick, which is about a six-hour drive. The next day, I do the last six. I'm too old to make all twelve hours in one day anymore"

I thought about what Sheriff Evans had said — that according to the medical examiner, Irene had been dead about two weeks before I found her. Gladys must have been one of the last people to have seen her alive.

"Well, let me give you some good news, Gladys. You need it." I told her about the testing and how the results seemed to be on target with what I'd predicted.

Gladys sighed, then began weeping again. "Isn't that always the way it goes? Here I am, planning the nicest and most comfortable retirement for Irene and me, and now she's gone. I thought I'd always have her with me."

I couldn't help it — tears welled in my eyes too. I blinked them away, rubbed her shoulder and suggested a bath or a nap, maybe. She opted for resting.

Tulip, who had been watching, trotted down the hall behind her to the guestroom and stayed with her until she fell asleep.

TWELVE

Gladys kept busy for the rest of the weekend with numerous calls to Sister to discuss Irene's funeral arrangements, and then making the funeral arrangements. She also insisted on helping with the daily cooking, which I agreed to only because it seemed to make her feel useful. It also gave me more time for paperwork.

By late Sunday I'd caught up and was ready to head back to the test site Monday morning. But before leaving I needed to pick up a few necessities at the drugstore. On the way out I found Gladys on the couch with Tulip, watching *Out of Africa* on the Oxygen Channel.

Shifting her attention from the movie, she said, "I got lucky."

"How's that?" I said.

"I figured the kids might be at the Sunday buffet at the Golden Corral today so I called home. Sure enough, no one answered and I was able to leave a message saying I was visiting a friend and would be home soon."

"Oh, good," I said. "What about the sheriff?"

"Got an appointment with him here tomorrow if that's all right with you."

"Of course it is. I won't be here, but you don't need me, do you?"

"No. I'll be fine. I gave him your address and he said he has one of those navigators in his car so it wouldn't be any trouble to find me. You just get back to the farm and finish our testing. That's the most important thing right now."

"Sounds like we have all the bases covered, then," I said and picked up my car keys.

In the drugstore, as the cashier counted out my change, I thought I saw Bud at the other end of the aisle. What was he doing at this drug store? He always used the small, family-owned drug store in his neighborhood, Country Club Hills.

More to the point, what was he doing in the condom section?

I took my bag and ducked out before Bud could see me. Then I jogged a block up the street to the only parking spot I'd been able to find, hopped in the Jeep and looked around for Bud's truck.

No sign of it. Instead I spotted his cream-colored Porsche Carrera and a hot young babe in it.

Bud pushed through the door of the drugstore, walked across the street and smiled — sheepishly, I thought — at the bimbo. They were laughing as the Porsche growled away from the curb, accelerated past me, and disappeared.

My throat constricted with emotions I couldn't identify. Jealousy? Possessiveness of my children's father? Common sense told me Bud hadn't been living these last five years as a monk, but this was my first time actually witnessing him moving on with his life. The intensity of my feelings surprised me. Indeed, considering I'd just crawled out of bed with another man, they were nonsensical. Still, I felt lousy, a little weird even. Then, being the practical person I am, I decided overanalyzing my emotions was a waste of time so I did what any level-headed, self-employed woman would do. I cranked up the tunes on the radio and headed back to the house to pack. Monday morning couldn't come soon enough for me.

I was back on the test site raring to go at seven o'clock, the faithful Tulip back by my side — at least she was until she caught the scent of some hapless critter and dashed off into the woods to find it. By ten we had finished the last few holes in the initial testing of the east side of the creek.

Mule and Stick were packing the last auger flights on the rig so we could move to the next one when Wink walked up and said, "Statewide just called. They're having some problems at a soil compaction test site about two hundred miles to the north —"

"Yeah, so?"

"Well, I'm the closest foreman in the area so I've been designated to take care of it."

"I see," I said. This was a normal occurrence, exploration companies often ran simple jobs without a foreman, calling in one only if there was a problem.

"Shouldn't take long to set whatever it is to right. Probably be back here by Wednesday night." Wink rolled out his field map, indicating a section of our site with his finger, and added, "This is the area you said you wanted to drill next, so I gave the boys their marching orders. Of course, you can change them if you want, but when they finish, it'll be time to move across the creek to test the west side of the property. This is the bridge we checked out, right here." He pointed to where he had circled the bridge on his map with a pencil.

"Sounds like a plan, don't worry about us," I reassured him. "We'll see you when you get back."

"Remember, if you need me and you can't reach me on the cell, it's because I'm in one of the dead zones down here. Just wait a little and try again."

"Gotcha," I said, absentmindedly, my thoughts skipping ahead to the moving drill rig.

I ran to catch up with the crew as the rig slowly bumped along through the woods on the newly cleared path.

By two o'clock we'd finished all the initial testing I had planned for the east side of the property. Now Mule and Stick stood by the rig waiting for instructions. Tulip sat at my feet looking up at me, waiting too.

"Let's head on across the creek," I said, reaching down to stroke one of her silky ears. She leaned into my knee and moaned happily. "We have plenty of daylight left to get set up on a core hole, maybe even pull one section before we knock off. I'll walk ahead of you."

The rich smell of raw earth and tree sap combined to delight my senses. It was better than perfume. I came to where the trail Wink had cleared dead ended into an old logging road, turned left, and followed it to the creek. As I crossed the twenty-foot earthen bridge, I took in the soothing sound of gurgling water as it flowed through the concrete culverts. Upon reaching the far side, I turned to watch my guys as they pulled up to the creek.

Both men got out to make a cursory check of the situation. Then Mule took the wheel as Stick, walking backwards and using hand signals, directed him forward until the front tires of the enormous rig were equally spaced on the edges of the narrow bridge. Now, with Stick still guiding him, Mule began to creep slowly across the creek.

I continued on my way to the drill flag. The sound of a woodpecker's hammer echoed again. Was it a red-bellied or a pileated . . . But then I heard a sickening crunch and panicked shouts from Stick.

"Hold it! Hold it! Hold it!" he hollered.

I turned and watched as the rig tilted dangerously to the left as that side of the bridge began to collapse under it in slow motion. "Noooo!" I screamed and ran back, my legs pumping like pistons.

In the few seconds it took me to reach the edge of the creek, the rig had almost reached its tipping point of forty-five degrees. Momentarily stopped, it hung motionless over the creek.

Mule sat behind the wheel like a crash dummy. The only thing moving was the water of the creek as it rushed around the rig's tires. All it would take would be a slight shift of the auger flights and the whole shooting match — rig, auger flights, and Mule — would go in the creek.

I watched the tires. The force of the water rushing around them was increasing in direct proportion to the volume now being trapped by the rig's position over the culverts. Angry swirls and eddies roiled in the once docile creek, chewing large chunks away from the earthen bridge. I understood it wasn't a question of if the rig would tip farther, but when.

Stick seemed to have arrived at the same conclusion and we both started screaming at Mule, "Get out! Get out!"

For a brief second he seemed glued to the wheel, but then he quickly got the message. He tried to distribute his weight evenly as he reached for the door. Stick ran to the cab to try to help him out.

With a clang, the auger flights shifted slightly and the rig sunk farther into the creek. The tilt was all that was needed to panic Mule into opening the driver's door and leaping out into the creek. Instantly, his feet were sucked from underneath him.

I caught a brief glimpse of his legs between the bottom of the door and the water before he disappeared with a gurgling yelp into the muddy cauldron.

At that moment the rig tipped beyond the point of no return and slowly began to settle itself in the creek. About half the load of auger flights unloaded into the water with a clamorous ring, like a madman loose in a belfry tower with a sledgehammer. The open door was the only thing that saved the rig from completely rolling over on its side.

"Mule!" I screamed and jumped in the creek. Water chunky with dirt, sticks, roots, and other debris from the collapsed earthen bridge beat against my legs as I waded to the door of the cab. I knew perfectly well it was a dumb thing to do, to go under a 25,000-pound drill rig — but I had to get Mule.

He was not going to drown on my watch. With the creek water swirling in a torrent around me, I pulled myself around the door, but then was sucked down and slammed into the undercarriage of the rig. When I came up, I found Mule. He'd been washed into the cab and was pinned flat against the passenger door by the force of the water.

With one hand I held on to the arm of the side-view mirror, and reached for Mule with my other. No good. It was all I could do to keep from getting trapped in the cab too. I pulled back and braced against the door, which was sinking deeper and deeper into the sandy creek bottom. At any moment the door was bound to buckle and the rig would lay completely down with Mule in it.

Stick now appeared, wading in from the back end of the truck. He grabbed me by the waist and pulled me back, yelling, "I'll get him!"

"No! Wait!" I yelled back with the sudden clarity often bestowed on the truly desperate. I looked into Mule's wild eyes. "Let go!" I shouted and made a waving motion with my hand toward the window. "Just go through the window!"

I saw realization dawn in his eyes, saw him take a deep breath and slip into the rushing torrent. I felt Stick push away from me. Then, for a second, the water level built up in the cab and the sucking pressure let up.

By the time I made it to the other side of the rig, Stick was hauling Mule onto what was left of the bridge. I hauled my soggy butt out of the creek. Tulip barked and leaped up and down like a pronghorn antelope. I realized she had been barking the whole time I was in the water.

"You okay?" I asked Mule.

"I think so," he said uncertainly. I didn't blame him for not knowing.

"Good. Get your ass on that dozer as fast as you can and push a channel through the bridge so the water won't beat to pieces what's left of it."

"Yes, ma'am," he said, heading off with Stick to get the bulldozer.

In less than ten minutes with the dozer they opened a channel and allowed the creek to settle back to being its lazy self. Only now, instead of bubbling over crayfish and flat rocks, it meandered through the rig — still propped on its door — and our scattered auger flights.

I stood on the creek bank and gazed at the wreck that was the rig. All I could see were winged dollar bills flying up and away from the carcass. The dozer clattered to a stop behind me and Mule and Stick came to stand beside me and survey the damage.

"Phew! That was a close one!" Stick exclaimed.

"You can say that again," Mule told him. "Good thing I've kept my girlish figure or I'd've never fit through that window."

"I can't believe you even tried to get out the down side of the rig in the first place, you moron. It's a damn miracle you weren't squished," Stick said.

"Don't be calling me a moron."

"And with the creek practically pushing you out the window, you still tried to come back out the driver's door. Don't you know the old saying, 'Go with the flow'?"

"Yeah. But haven't you ever heard the one about, 'Never leave through a different door than the one you came in'?"

"Knock it off, you two," I said. "Truth be told, the open door's the only thing that's keeping the rig from tipping over completely. Start stripping off the auger flights, casings, and anything else that isn't attached to the rig."

"We got enough chains in Stick's truck to reach from the dozer to the rig, but I don't think we'll have enough horsepower to pull it out," Mule said.

"You're right," I said, "we won't. Besides, I'm afraid we'd break the rig in half, pulling from the bank. Angle's too steep. We need an all-terrain wrecker, something with flotation tires so it can get down in the creek and work from a better angle. I think I know where to get one."

It took me several tries before I was able to reach Wink's voicemail. I dreaded giving him the bad news that way, so just left a message to call me. With luck, I'd have the rig up and in a garage with repairs underway

before he called me back.
   Make that lots and lots of luck.

THIRTEEN

I drove straight to a truck garage I'd seen at the edge of the small town of Stella off Highway 17. I'd noticed it because it seemed a large operation for such a small town and therefore I suspected it specialized in tractor repairs. Which meant they had wreckers big enough to haul tractors. I stepped from the Jeep, noticing that, for the second time in two weeks, my clothes had dried on my body due to a dunking on the job. I tried to brush away dried silt and bits of grass and roots as I made my way across a large concrete parking area and stepped into the cool shade of one of three large work bays.

Several large tractors, looking like giant wounded crustaceans, were being attended to, hoods removed, mechanics on either side working intently. The place smelled of motor oil and sweat. Hydraulic wrenches whirled and bursts of compressed air hissed from hoses snaking in every direction. I threaded my way through these obstacles, headed for the office.

A round-faced middle-aged woman with teased black hair glanced up from where she pounded away on an ancient adding machine. Even when she stopped punching numbers in, the machine clicked and whirred away as if it was totaling up the national debt.

"What can I do for you, honey?" she asked. Instantly I felt a little better and explained my problem.

"Lordy, honey. What you need is *Sweet Thang.*"

" '*Sweet Thang'?*" I repeated dubiously.

She pointed to a photo on the wall of a very shiny electric blue wrecker with flotation tires, each of which would reach my shoulders. The photo appeared to have been taken at some type of tractor pull or truck rodeo. SWEET THANG was emblazoned across the side of the wrecker in bold yellow shadow script.

"Wow!" was all I could think to say.

"That's my Jimmy's pride and joy. Jimmy's my husband. Let me call him for you, honey," said Ms. Jimmy. Without leaving her rolling chair, she scooted to a door behind her gray steel desk, opened it and yelled,

"Jimmy!" When he didn't respond in the next nanosecond, she said, "Be right back," and sprang up to find him.

A few minutes later, I heard a clattering roar and *Sweet Thang* rumbled around the corner of the building looking just as it did in the photo.

Jimmy pulled the wrecker up in front of where I stood — I was wrong, the tires actually reached to my chin — and climbed out. "Jimmy Purdue," he said with an out-stretched hand.

"Cleo Cooper," I said. "Glad to meet you."

His wife came out of the office door and stood beside me as he continued, "Melva tells me you're in a fine mess and need some help right now."

"She told you right. Can you help me?"

"Well." He squinted up at the sun. "It's about four. We probably have enough light, but we need to get moving. We got bingo at church tonight. Starts at eight and I'm the caller."

"I understand," I said. "Follow me."

I jumped back in the Jeep and drove to the site with *Sweet Thang* chained down to a rollback carrier plus an empty carrier right behind me. My luck got even better when Jimmy told me that the situation wasn't as bad as it looked. Since the rig hadn't completed a 90-degree flip, the oil didn't run out of the engine block. According to Jimmy, that was a good thing. Apparently.

I'm pretty good with large machines as far as how they do what I need on a worksite, but their mysterious inner workings will always remain, well, mysterious to me.

In less than two hours, Jimmy and *Sweet Thang* had the rig pulled out of the creek and loaded on the carrier, and he was on his way back to town for bingo night. The crew, having no rig to drill with, headed for their motel.

My cell clanged. Wink. Perfect timing.

After I told him what had happened, we made plans to meet at Purdue's Garage late the next afternoon, check on the repairs, and formulate a plan to get the testing back on track as fast as possible. When I suggested maybe even getting another rig to the site if Statewide had one available, Wink didn't make noises as if that was a total impossibility. I was just starting to feel like my mojo was still working. Then my cell phone rang again. I checked the screen. Gladys.

"Gladys, what's up?" I said.

"Cleo? Is that you?" Her voice trembled and she sounded disoriented.

"You okay, Gladys?"

"Well, I don't know . . ."

"What's the matter?"

"Well, I talked to that nice sheriff and right after he left, the children drove up. How did they know I was here?"

My guess: they followed the sheriff. I closed my eyes and rubbed my now aching head." I'm not sure," I lied.

"Me either." Gladys sighed. "Anyway, they're both here, saying they want me to come home with them. I told them no, but they brought out that old paper they want me to sign again. They're in the kitchen now, waiting for me. I'm feeling a little dizzy. I think I've had too big of a day."

"Where are you now?" I asked, worried. She sounded so vulnerable.

"In the powder room. I told them I didn't feel good. I know they don't mean any harm. I just can't seem to make them understand that they can't push me around and now . . . now I feel so tired . . ."

"Gladys. Listen to me very carefully," I said slowly and deliberately. "Go upstairs to my bedroom. Open the door to the deck and go out to the little gate that leads to the private stairs and the garden below. Open it too. Leave both the gate and the bedroom door open. Understand?"

"Yes."

"Then go to my walk-in closet. Look to the left at floor level. You'll see a small access panel that leads to the ceiling over the side porch. It has a magnetic fastener like a kitchen cabinet. When I first moved in by myself, I rigged it so I'd always have a hiding place. Just tap the panel and it will open. Crawl through and lock it with the slide bolt on the other side. Understand?"

"I think so," she said hesitantly.

"See," I explained, "when Robert Earle and Shirley come looking for you, they'll see the door and the gate open and think you've gone outside. They can look for you all they want. They'll never find you as long as you stay quiet. You said you were tired. Take a nap. There'll be a nice breeze through the eaves."

"Okay. Open the doors and crawl through the little panel door in the closet. I'm so sorry for all this . . ."

I interrupted her. "Don't worry, Gladys. I'll be right there. Just stay cool. Everything's going to be all right."

Almost exactly two hours later, at the edge of twilight, Tulip and I dashed up the stairs to my house. We were met at my front door by Robert Earle, who jerked it open in my face.

"What are you doing here?" Had he somehow failed to notice it was my house?

A startled Tulip burst into a staccato barrage of barking, her jaws snapping like a furry crocodile. I grabbed her collar before she could lunge teeth-first into his crotch.

"Down, girl!" I said to Tulip. "Sit." She subsided begrudgingly, her eyes glued to her quarry.

"That's a question more properly put to you, Robert Earle," I said.

"We came to see Mom," Shirley said, emerging from the side of the house. Both of them appeared sweaty and winded.

I swept past them into the living room, a still uneasy Tulip following close on my heels. There I noticed a large arrangement of tropical lilies and roses sitting on the coffee table. No Gladys, thankfully. In the kitchen, I sat my keys on the stove island and looked around.

Relieved Gladys wasn't there either, I said casually, "So where is your mother?"

"Oh, like you don't know. We've been looking for her almost two hours —"

Shirley interrupted, "We were having a nice little chat and then all of a sudden she got up to go upstairs and now we can't find her. The door to your deck upstairs is open. We think she may have wandered outside and gotten disoriented . . . you know, she's old and gets confused easily."

"Yeah," Robert Earle chimed in.

"Translation," I said, "you two were trying to coerce her into signing your Power of Attorney papers — yet again — and any disorientation she might be experiencing is from whatever tranquilizer you gave her."

"Well! I never!" Shirley sputtered. "We . . . we would never do anything that might hurt our mother or force her to do anything of the kind. We just want her home."

"Glad to hear it. In that case, I'm sure she just walked up to Cameron Village for a little shopping."

I opened the front door and waved them through it. "When she gets back, I'll tell her you guys had to go."

Brother and sister stomped down my front steps. Before reaching the sidewalk, Robert Earle turned and growled, "You aren't taking what's ours."

He was getting pretty predictable, I must say.

"I'm not taking anything. I'm paying the rightful owner, your mother, for it. Y'all have a nice day now, you hear," I said and firmly closed the door.

I unlaced my field boots, which were coated in dried creek mud, pulled them off, then trotted quickly through the house to the back door and opened it a crack. In a few minutes, I heard Robert Earle's Escalade crank up down the street. He and Shirley had parked around the block so their mother wouldn't see them drive up. I went back to the front window and watched them cruise slowly by the house before they drove off.

Then I ran to my bedroom, ducked under the hanging clothes, and pushed the panel. Though I was expecting it to be locked, a moment of panic seized me when it didn't open. What if she was unconscious on the other side? How would I reach her? Rip open the door with a crowbar? Reining in my runaway fears, I rapped lightly on the door and called out, "Open up, Gladys, it's me."

For a few seconds there was only silence. I bit my knuckle as my anxiety mounted. Then, in a voice much stronger than the one I'd heard two hours ago, Gladys said, "Who's *me*?"

I laughed with relief. "Cleo Cooper. Open up."

"Oh, thank the good lord," Gladys said, opening the door and crawling through.

"Breeze or not, it's kinda warm up here."

We stood up together, me holding her lightly by her shoulders to steady her, as she still seemed a little woozy.

"Come on downstairs," I said. "The coast is clear."

I made her a nice cup of oolong tea. Gladys sat on a stool and sipped.

"How do you feel now?" I asked.

"Kind of like I used to after a night of one-fifty-proof daiquiris and three packs of Marlboros." We both laughed.

Then her face darkened. "I hate to admit it to anyone — including myself — but I think the kids might've drugged me." Her chin trembled. "I keep asking myself over and over, what did I do to ever make them feel I'm incapable of taking care of myself? Especially considering the fact that I've been the one taking care of them all these years. Hell, those two have never lifted a finger or asked to be involved in any way and now . . . now they think they need to take over?"

What could I say? If I knew anything at all, it was that I could say anything about my children, but no one else better do it. I patted her hand, got up, and rooted around in the pantry until I found a bag of Nutter Butters.

"When things seem really screwed up and confused, eat a cookie," I said. "It'll all come clear sooner or later."

I munched a cookie, savoring its salty sweetness and said, "You know, Gladys, I've been thinking it might be best to move you someplace the kids would never think of looking. They obviously know where I live now."

"Oh, my dear, I'm sure you had no idea how much trouble my family and I would be when you started this project. Lord knows, I didn't either. I just feel terrible about this . . ."

"It's no trouble and I think I might know just the place. But let me make a phone call first. Be right back." I went upstairs to my bedroom for privacy. I was pretty sure I could count on Bud, but what with the new little girlfriend . . . I dialed his cell, told him what I needed and why. I could tell he was delighted to have me asking for another favor.

He said, "Of course you can use the beach house, Cleo. You know you can use anything I have, anytime."

Really? Does that include the pretty young thing I saw you with yesterday? I could use a good cleaning woman. "I appreciate that," I said, in prudent mode. "I'll take her up tomorrow and it will just be until I finish testing and can wrap up this project legally."

"No problem. Take as long as you need. Maybe you'll cook me dinner again one night real soon. Maybe even throw in some dessert."

I clamped my bottom lip firmly between my teeth.

"Did I say something wrong?" he said in reaction to my silence.

"No." Prudence spoke for me again. "I'm just tired. I had an accident on the site today —"

"Damn! Was anyone hurt? Will you have to deal with OSHA now?"

"Uh, no, to the first question and yes to the second, but OSHA won't get the reports until after we're through. I figure we'll finish up this week, but, look, I don't have time to go into all this right now. Just thanks again for the use of the house, Bud. Gotta go."

I could hear him starting to ask if I wanted to get together and talk about it as I closed my cell.

FOURTEEN

Gladys didn't seem to mind when I hustled her out the next morning, Tuesday, like I was the Mad Hatter and we were late for the tea party. I practically threw her and her bags into the Jeep. Tulip, ever ready, leaped into her spot in the back as soon as I cracked open the door. By seven o'clock we were on our way to Bud's beach house. At best, it would be ten by the time I got her settled in.

Noticing my clammy palms and that I had a death grip on the wheel, I took a deep breath and reminded myself that stress causes wrinkles. I gripped the wheel harder.

"Something wrong, dear?" asked Gladys.

"No, not at all. Just lots to do. I've got to meet with my banker later today in New Bern — just thinking about that . . . Would you like some music?" I said, indicating my iPod playlist.

Gladys scanned it. "Oh goody, Metallica."

Dear lord. Henri had complied the playlist for me, hence Metallica. Thank goodness for earbuds. I handed them over to her.

We were nearly there when Gladys removed the ear buds and sighed loud enough that I knew something was on her mind. "What we were talking about yesterday, Cleo . . . The kids trying to get me to sign a Power of Attorney or have me committed or whatever . . ."

"Yes, yes, I remember," I urged her on.

"I'm embarrassed by their behavior and at the same time, I question myself. Maybe I'm overreacting. Maybe I should go home and tackle the issue head on and get this behind me."

"Is that what you want to do?"

She sighed. "Not really. The older I get, the more I try to avoid scenes and unpleasantness at all costs. Also, they're continually pointing out how forgetful I am, showing me little things around the house I haven't done. Things I know I did, like turn off the sprinkler or the television or the stove. After awhile, it can get to you and you start getting confused. Sometimes I've . . . well, I've even thought they're trying to gaslight me because when I'm by myself, I don't forget things. But then, they are my children. They wouldn't do that . . ."

149

Gladys gloomily looked out the window as neat rows of lush corn blinked by, then turned back to me and said bluntly, "A few days at home with them and I feel like I belong in a nuthouse."

"Gladys," I said, "let me tell you a quick story about a lovely, gentle, little black lady — Opal was her name. I met her when I worked for GeoTech. She owned a small five-acre parcel of land near New Bern, which was in a line of similar-size parcels that backed up to GeoTech's property in that area. They were actively mining the marine limestone in that area in a dragline operation called slot mining, and it was my job to purchase all those parcels of land as the dragline came within reach of them.

"Now, the dragline is an enormous excavating crane. This Jeep would easily fit into its bucket. It is so big, in fact, that it can only mine the land directly within the reach of its boom. The bucket drops from the end of the boom and as cables drag it back toward the crane, it scoops up tons of limestone and leaves a slot. Hence the name. After the slot is mined out, the dragline is moved backwards in a complicated and time-consuming operation to the next location.

"Point is, once the dragline has gone past

a location, there's no returning for small parcels. Opal's children thought GeoTech was out to cheat her. They convinced her to hold out for more money. No amount of proof I showed her about what the other landowners had been paid or logic on my part could persuade her that she needed to take the deal offered her.

"I think she really wanted to, but her children pressured her to the point that she got confused. Anyway, the dragline moved on and left her parcel of land behind. A year later, the company flooded that section and left her sitting on a little peninsula of land in a five-hundred-acre lake."

"Did she continue to live there?"

"For a while. Her original plan was to buy a small house in town from the proceeds of the land sale. Make life easier for herself. But because she took her children's advice, she couldn't. I felt sorry for her, and at the time I was divorcing Bud and needed a place of peace and quiet, a hideaway, if you will. So I bought the parcel from her. She took the money this time and got to move into town after all."

"Opal . . . Did she ever sell daffodils out by the dirt road that ran in front of her house?"

"Yes. She did," I said, amazed. "How did

you know that?"

"Irene loved her flower stand. How she knew about it, I don't know, since it was way back off the main highway. Every spring, we'd make a trek to a favorite tackle shop of hers down that way. She was quite the fisherman, you know. On the way back, we'd always leave the highway, wind back through the woods on those sandy dirt roads — I was always scared we'd get stuck — and buy jars and jars of those daffodils. I can smell them now . . ."

Gladys grew silent. I patted her hand on the console and said, "I didn't mean to make you sad. I was only trying to point out how once you get yourself in a situation where you control your destiny, you'll be much happier and you'll never question your sanity again. You can trust your own judgment."

"I know you're right. I guess I'm just impatient to get to that point."

"We'll get there," I said. "Don't you worry. And speaking of getting there, here we are."

Bud's family had been part of the South since before the Revolutionary War. A large family, they had spread from Georgia to North Carolina and amassed great wealth growing, selling, and ginning cotton until the 1950s, when they diversified into other, even more profitable areas. Back in the 1930s, Bud's grandparents bought the house on Wrightsville Beach that now sat before Gladys and me. It was nestled among other grand old dames built during a time when planning and zoning boards allowed for construction right behind what's called the fore-dune ridge, the leading line of sand dunes before reaching the beach proper.

Seahaven was a stately three-story house made of weathered cypress. Its bright, orange-red canvas awnings had to be replaced every ten years or so unless a hurricane blew them away first. It was situated facing the ocean on the third of three inline lots. The first two were empty except for a parking area by the road and a long wooden boardwalk that skimmed the tops of the dunes. I'd fallen in love with the house's quiet dignity and endearing charm the first time I'd seen it and have to say that it is the only trapping of a wealthy marriage that I missed.

Just like me, Gladys was thrilled by Seahaven, which made it easier to leave her there alone to explore it. She'd have Tulip as her companion. In fact, the arrangement worked out well for Tulip. I'd been worried about her recovery progress and yesterday's excitement with the bridge couldn't be what the doctor ordered. More time off was the therapy Tulip really needed.

After I made sure they were well settled in, I got back in the Jeep and checked my cell before heading for New Bern. Damn. Wink had called but left no message. A twinge of anxiety crept up my spine. Why was he trying to reach me? Was there going to be a serious delay in testing? I tried to return his call. When he didn't answer, I simply closed my cell. Whatever the problem, I'd see him this afternoon. Right now it was time to fight another battle: a meeting with my banker.

Like a lot of women who divorce after a decades-long marriage, I found that most of my friends went with my marriage. Lonnie Harris, my banker, was an exception. He'd remained neutral. When I approached him with a loan request to start a quarry, he was sincere about wanting to see my business plan. After he saw it — which, if my geology proved correct, would net his bank a tidy profit — he was glad to lend me the cash I needed.

In truth, poor Lonnie was desperately trying to steer his small independent bank through the treacherous waters of bank failures and bailouts that ruled the day. To accomplish that, he needed to think out of the box while still maintaining the number one rule of banking: only make loans that are sure bets with big returns.

Right now, everything was contingent on the geologic data. I'd figured on another week to get what I needed to calculate the volume of rock available for mining and back it up with core samples. Because of the delay with the overturned rig, I was a little worried I wouldn't make it. Yet, I had faith in Wink. Together, we'd figure something out.

I joined Lonnie at his golf club, and from the beginning of the meeting in the clubhouse restaurant, I could sense that he was a little reserved, not his usual jovial self. He didn't even perk up when I told him I was right on schedule and would be ready the first of next week with a presentation for his bosses. I figured there was no sense bothering him with frivolous details about overturned rigs and delays.

As I went through the information I thought Lonnie ought to know, he'd nod his head occasionally or readjust his position in the tan leather booth. When I finished, he quietly promised he'd take care of rounding up all the big wigs that needed to be there. And then he let me know what was bothering him.

"Cleo, I've known you for a very long time and you're a very smart woman, but . . ."

"But what? I knew there was something."

"But business is business," he said, swallowing hard. "And I was thinking — is there any way you could get Bud —"

"Lonnie, stop right there. I've put everything I have into your past assurances that you and your bank would be looking forward to working with *me* — not my former husband or his family — on this project. And, I might add, making a large profit for the privilege."

"That was before over three hundred banks failed nationwide, Cleo. Globally — well, I don't even know how many. Hell, this is the deepest recession since the Great Depression. Damn it. There's no credit flowing anywhere." He slumped back in his chair.

I glared at him. I didn't care if my homicidal impulses showed on my face.

Shaking his head, Lonnie said, "For Christ's sake . . . I'm not saying no, you know."

"No?"

"It's just that everything, and I mean *everything,* has to be to the bank's benefit.

Times ten. There cannot be the slightest risk for us. Do you understand?"

"There won't be. I told you that months ago," I said, and stood up before he could say anything else. "So we're still on for next week's meeting?"

"Yes," he said, barely looking at me. "I'll call you with the time. And that brings me to another thing. You positively have to have your presentation ready by Tuesday."

"Why?"

"Because the executives required to approve the four-million-dollar term loan will be down here that day on another matter. Trust me, Cleo, in times like these, we'll need to include your project with several others, rather than have it considered alone."

Moving my agenda up by several days after everything that had happened? Gosh, no pressure there. I looked down at my nervous banker as he finger-combed his prematurely thinning salt and pepper hair.

"Right. Always a pleasure, Lonnie," I said. As I stormed out, trying to appear casual, all I could think was that Wink better have some good news for me.

FIFTEEN

Traffic was bad. The trip from New Bern to the garage in Stella was going to take at least an hour. If I tried real hard, I might be able to calm down before I got there. I was just about to put in another call to Wink when my cell vibrated. Bud.

"Yes?" I said impatiently.

"I completely forgot that Will is coming up at the end of the week and wants to stay at Seahaven for a while. Do you think your friend would mind some company?"

"I knew about this, and she's looking forward to meeting him."

"Good, uh . . ."

I didn't have time for him to pause and collect his thoughts. "I'm listening, Bud."

"Well, it's just that I want you to know I'm always here for . . ."

"Oops!" I interrupted him as I heard a beep for another call coming in. "Gotta go!" I clicked over to the other call, from Will.

"Hey, Mom. Just calling to let you know I got a lucky break. You remember my friend from Wake Forest, Joe? The one whose dad has a private plane?"

"Of course I do."

"Well, he's coming down here Thursday to pick up Joe for a trip home and he said he'll give me a ride and drop me off anywhere along the way."

"Great," I said. "Tell him to drop you at a little strip called Albert J. Ellis Airport. That's close to my worksite and Seahaven too. I'll pick you up. Just give me a call or text me to let me know when."

"Will do," he said.

Spotting a Jiffy Mart gas station jammed between a Mexican food store and a Laundromat, I pulled over and availed myself of the ladies' room. As soon as I stepped out, Shirley's boyfriend appeared in front of me.

"Oops," I said, avoiding a collision with him.

"Hey there . . ." he said.

"Uh. Hello."

I stood there for a moment but when he didn't offer any explanation as to why he was lurking outside the ladies' room, I said, "We've really got to stop meeting like this, Ivan."

He gave a fake little snort. "I saw you pull

in here and thought I'd take the opportunity to ask you to reconsider your position on letting Shirley see her mother."

I sighed. "Tell your girlfriend I don't have anything to do with what Gladys does or who she sees. She's a grown woman."

He snorted again only this time sarcastically. "Listen, Shirley's going to be my wife. I'll be taking care of her from now on and let me tell you, I take that responsibility very seriously. You hurt her or anyone in her family and you'll have me to deal with. You got that?" He punctuated his last sentence with an index finger held a few inches from my nose.

Several remarks regarding this rude body language occurred to me. Mostly ones referring to Ivan's mental soundness or lack thereof, but I decided against voicing any of them.

"Gee, it's getting late," I said instead. "I've got to run."

Unfortunately I had to take the time to fill the Jeep's tank. I watched Ivan get into a mud-spattered, silver Dodge Ram 4×4.

As he exited the parking lot, he scraped the tire in a poorly executed right-hand turn. Clearly this guy belonged right up there with Robert Earle and Shirley when it came to creepy.

Change in plans. Wink and I were still missing each other with our calls, but he had left another message, this time telling me to skip Purdue's and meet him at the site. My stomach twisted in again. Did that mean he'd already been to Purdue's and found the rig's repairs were going to take weeks instead of days? Were no other rigs available? Was the crew at the site now packing up the equipment to leave? I needed that data in order to be ready for the Big Bankers by Tuesday or this whole operation was sunk. I raced there as fast as I could, driving the Jeep through the woods to the site this time, ignoring the limbs scratching the sides.

My anxiety evaporated as I stepped from the Jeep and saw a repaired earthen bridge and a drill rig on the other side busily chewing out a fresh core sample from my granite deposit. Mule and Stick waved as I strode past them to where Wink stood by his pickup filling in data on his field map.

"Dang, Wink," I said. "There's no gum on your shoes!"

He chuckled. "No sense wasting time. Soon's you told me about the accident, I got on the horn with our dispatcher and for a while there, I thought we might be up the creek without a paddle, but he scrounged around and came up with that raggedy-ass backup rig. I know the boys that run that concrete plant right outside Jacksonville. Great guys. They practically beat me out here with three new culverts. Didn't take long to push a little dirt over them and get a road back across the creek. Got something to show you, though," he said as he walked around to the passenger door of his pickup, opened it and removed one of several pieces of concrete from the floorboard. He pointed to a small smooth curved spot along its jagged edge. "See this?" he said.

"Yeah?" I said.

"It's a piece of pipe from that bridge out there."

I took the concrete from his hand and inspected it. "That's weird. It looks like . . ."

"Like a drill hole," he said, finishing my thought. But I didn't even know I'd been thinking it. I just knew there was something wrong with what I was seeing.

"Listen," Wink said. "It looks to me like somebody came out here with a cordless heavy-duty drill and honeycombed that concrete pipe. S'why it collapsed."

"Are you sure?"

"You and I both checked that bridge. Don't know about you, but I climbed inside and there were no holes there then."

He was right. We'd both inspected it Friday morning.

"Considering someone's already tampered with the core boxes and now this happens. Well, kinda looks like someone wants you to give up and leave," Wink said grimly.

"Or run me out of money," I said.

"That too, but, whoever it was, they didn't cost you as much as they might have hoped. Damage to the rig is minimal, mostly cosmetic. Then there's the cost of a couple of concrete pipes — that's not much."

"Could have been catastrophic, though," I said.

"Yeah, if the drill had flopped over or if anyone'd been hurt . . ."

We quietly contemplated that possibility. "Oh yeah, before I forget." Wink reached in the back pocket of his jeans and gave me a crumpled scrap of paper with a telephone number scratched on it. "Sheriff dropped by earlier today looking for you. Said to give him a call at that number."

I looked at the paper. "Thanks" I said, noticing by the prefix that it wasn't the sheriff's office number; probably his cell.

"You going to tell him about this?" Wink

asked, holding up the piece of pipe.

"I'm not sure if that would be a good idea. I'm under a lot of pressure from my banker to wrap up all our results in a shiny New York-style presentation by next Tuesday, seven days from now. My son — he's designing the computer presentation for me — needs the data by Friday. Even skipping some of the drill holes and taking a few less cores, it's going to be a stretch."

And that wasn't the only reason. I was hating this conversation.

"Listen Wink, you don't need to be concerned about anything, but just in case the sheriff shows up out here again, there is the possibility that he is starting to think Irene Mizzell's murder and all the hard luck I've been having out here might somehow be connected. If he's spooked, he could order us to shut down until he finds out who killed Irene. If he does that, I'm done. No way I can make my presentation without that data. And without the presentation, there's no money. No money . . . well, guess you can figure the rest."

Wink pulled at his bottom lip. "Well, we could stretch the distance between drill holes and leave out a couple. What's the word . . . we could extrapa . . ."

"Extrapolate? Fudge it?"

164

"Yeah, that's it. Fudge it."

"As it happens," I said confidently, "I'm pretty good at fudging it, so go ahead, drop the depth-check on every other hole unless absolutely necessary and cut the number of cores from every other hole to every third hole. Meantime, I'll check in with the sheriff, see what he wants. I'm going to leave out the bridge collapse. No sense worrying the law with stuff we can handle ourselves, right?"

"Right," said Wink, looking a little overwhelmed.

A few quick directions from the sheriff led me straight to what he referred to as his secret fishing hole. Though I'd never fished it myself, I knew exactly where it was from years of prospecting in the area. Ever since people started building roads down east, they have used the limestone marl dug from shallow depths as base material. After a mining operation ceases, the irregular depression that results fills with water, making a wonderful fishing and swimming hole. These ponds also served as reservoirs for wildlife and people during times of drought.

As I joined Sheriff Evans at his favorite spot, I wondered why he felt seeing me was important enough to interrupt a good worm-drowning.

"There's an extra rod in the bed of the pickup, if you want to wet a hook."

"No, thanks," I said. "I'm content to just watch you."

"Suit yourself. I'll get right to the crux of the matter. I'm a little concerned about you and your crew."

"How's that?" I asked trying to sound casual.

He wiped his brow with his sleeve and cast his line before he said, "My detectives, along with crime scene investigators, have pretty well determined that the black plastic grill cover Miz Mizzell was wrapped in more than likely came off the one on the back porch of Gladys Walton's house. Both the grill and the cover are the same make, Coleman. This brings the Walton kids back under some strong scrutiny."

"Isn't that a commonly used brand?" I asked, playing devil's advocate.

He pulled a little more line from his reel, watching the action of the silk fly as he teased it along the surface of the pond. "There's more."

"Oh?"

"Yeah. After looking at recent photos of Miz Mizzell, it's plain that her resemblance to her cousin is significant. Because forensics placed the location of the murder in the kitchen of Miz Walton's home" — he interrupted himself to take a swipe at the sweat on his brow again — "and, in light of the information you gave me regarding the Walton kids inheriting their mom's estate, it's our feeling right now that Miz Mizzell was murdered by mistake. The real target was Gladys Walton."

I adjusted my Ray Bans and hoped the shiver that traveled through my body upon hearing an officer of the law voice my suspicions had gone unnoticed.

The sheriff reeled in and made another cast. "Shirley has a very solid alibi for the time surrounding our best estimate of when Miz Mizzell died. She was in Raleigh at a week-long high school reunion. She was on some of the committees, helped plan some of the activities. It all checks out. That leaves Robert Earle as our main suspect. I know he's made repeated trips to your worksite, which brings us back to you and your crew out there on the Walton land."

Uh-oh.

"You got any more information you want to offer?" he asked.

I felt like I had to give him something. "Well, Robert Earle did try to take over testing the property with a phony contract from a company I never heard of. He claimed to have a Power of Attorney, but, when I pushed him, he couldn't produce it."

I could see a fresh coating of sweat appear on the sheriff's forehead. After a long moment, he said, "You should tell me things like this. This could be important to our investigation. We'll definitely want to talk to Gladys again." He punctuated his sentence with a cast that sent his fly clear to the other side of the pond where it settled into the murky water under the overhang of a limestone boulder.

Crap. I had a sinking feeling I wouldn't be able to keep her location from him, although I was going to give it my best shot. I decided to start with a tactic that's rarely failed me, the guilt trip.

"About that," I said. "I had to move her. Robert Earle and Shirley found Gladys by following you to my house. It upset her pretty bad."

This time the sheriff's head snapped around so hard I'm pretty sure I saw sweat fly from under his chin. "You should have told me that too." His right hand had gone to his hip, his rod all but forgotten in his left. "All of the information you're giving me right now goes to motive, and, frankly, it suggests that Gladys Walton could be in real danger. Where the hell is she? She may need police protection."

So much for guilt-tripping him.

"Now, Sheriff Evans," I said in my most soothing voice, taking a dignified stance with hands clasped behind my back. "There's absolutely no reason to do that. Besides, you know a little about Gladys and understand how very headstrong and proud she is. She's also in denial about her children having anything to do with Irene's death and, quite naturally, she doesn't want to believe they might do anything to hurt her.

"That little incident with them trying to get her to sign a Power of Attorney did get her attention, however, and she now knows better than to answer the phone until I get all the testing completed and our legal affairs finalized."

"Where the hell is she?" he said through clenched teeth. Apparently, my quiet professional bearing was unappreciated by Sheriff Evans.

"She told me not to say." My voice sounded like an embarrassing faint echo of its normal volume.

"You own a gun, Miz Cooper?" The giant, sweaty sheriff was now looming over me.

His fishing rod abandoned. "Answer me," he said.

"Yes sir," I said.

"Where is it?"

"In my Jeep. Why?"

"Let me see it. Now."

I quickly retrieved my Beretta 380 and handed it to him.

"You got a permit to carry concealed?"

"No," I said, trying to sound confident. "I don't need one as long as I inform any law officer upon being pulled over —"

"I'm familiar with the rules, Miz Cooper." He handed my gun back to me.

"Mind if I ask what kind of gun was used to kill Irene?"

Sheriff Evans crossed his arms and widened his stance. "Mind telling me where Gladys Walton is?"

It was no use. I caved. "She's at my ex-husband's beach house on Wrightsville Beach. My dog's with her and my son's coming in on Thursday. No one, other than my ex-husband and now you, knows where she is. I'm sure we can keep it that way." I gave him my best lopsided smile.

Sheriff Evans looked at my gun again and said, "The bullet removed from Miz Mizzell's skull was a .22. And, as for the reason I wanted to know if you had a gun, considering the kind of situation we're dealing with here, you may need it. And let me warn you now, I'm just about a hair's-breadth away from closing down your testing site until we wrap up this case."

I looked stricken, probably suicidal. Sheriff Evans shook his head. "I'll call you soon as I decide the best way for me to meet with Miz Walton again."

All I could do was nod. It wasn't as if I hadn't been expecting it, but I still needed a tumbler of Jack Black, pronto. Maybe two.

Sixteen

All the crap that was screwing up my project — Irene's murder, keeping Gladys hidden from her children, that overprotective moose of a sheriff — had me too wired to let the alcohol do its work. Add to that my skittish banker, Lonnie, pushing up my completion date from very difficult to nearly impossible, and you've got a recipe for nervous breakdown, not a whiskey on the rocks.

I longed for someone to talk to, but Tulip was playing guard dog for Gladys. Maybe catching up with Henri would have the soothing, lulling effect I was looking for. Thirty minutes later I was still listening to her wrestle with such monumental decisions as which shoes at Monkey's 50-percent-off sale went best with her current wardrobe. There was also that perennial favorite of how much longer she was going to let the latest testosterone-laden guy in her life pant before making it perfectly clear he was never going to make it to the Promised Land.

"I mean, I don't care how hot he is, how can you get worked up about a tax accountant, Mom?"

"I can see where that'd be a problem," I said just as another call beeped in. Nash Finley. Without missing a beat, I cut Henri off in mid-sentence, "I need to catch this. Business!"

"What's up, Nash?" I asked nonchalantly.

"Me. I'm in the air en route to the beach. Are you anywhere near the Albert J. Ellis Airport?"

"As a matter of fact, I am."

"Good. Can you pick me up there in about an hour?"

I checked my watch and tried to dampen the surge of energy that rushed through me. *Easy, girl.* I still wasn't in any way sure I wanted a relationship with him. Flashbacks of our white hot sex gave me the idea that a little sex was just what I needed right now to take my mind off business troubles.

"You still there?" he asked in response to my deadening silence of indecision.

"Where's your car?"

"At Wrightsville Beach, at the Blockade Runner. Safety Department had a seminar there for North and South Carolina quar-

173

ries, and one of the foreman, Billy — you remember him?"

"Yes, I know Billy."

"Well, he drove my car down from Raleigh and was supposed to leave it at the airport for me. But something got mixed up and he left it at the hotel. Anyway, before I made other arrangements, I thought I'd check with you." Then, his voice lowered, took on a playful tone, and he added, "I'll make sure you're well compensated for your trouble."

Maybe it was my old buddy, Jack Daniel's. Maybe it was my hormones. Or maybe it was a thumb of the nose to Bud and the young bimbo. Whatever the reason, I said, "Sure, Nash. I'll pick you up."

I showered and dressed in a pair of creamy linen slacks and a crisp, white sleeveless blouse. I pinned my hair up loosely with a tortoise-shell clip, the tension between tailored and tousled being the idea.

Ellis Airport lies just northwest of the town of Stella and about fifty minutes from Wrightsville. I got there a little early, so had time to indulge myself watching private planes taking off and landing. I grew up on *Dallas* and *Dynasty.* If Mattel had made a Barbie corporate jet, I would have had one. In hot pink, to match the RV.

A particularly sleek little Cessna Conquest set down on the runway like a fairy tern on a calm sea and taxied to the hangar about fifty yards from where I stood. I leaned against a corner of the terminal building behind a cyclone fence and watched, blinking in the bright glare of the sun. Should have brought my shades.

Nash got out, followed by the pilot. He fussed with his bag as the pilot moved into the shade under the wing of the plane. When he waved, I waved back, losing sight of his companion, who headed into the hangar. Nash was carrying only a small overnight bag as he followed me to the Jeep.

Blue crab claws and grilled pork tenderloin at the Port Land Grille — delicious. What followed was . . . well, let's just characterize Nash's remarkable set of skills as potentially life-threatening, as I worried my heart couldn't take all the exertion.

Afterward, as we lounged on the balcony of his ocean-view room listening to the surf pound the beach, my mind was everywhere but on the romance of the moment. Particularly troubling to me was the fact that the sheriff had also suspected Irene was killed because she looked like Gladys. I resisted looking at my watch; I knew it was too late to run by and see Gladys. Wasn't there some way I could move this project along faster? For everyone's safety.

Nash startled me when he took my hand, kissed my palm, and said, "Did you like my flowers?"

"Flowers?"

"The ones I sent to your house in Raleigh — so they'd arrive on Monday? . . . You know, after we were together on Friday."

And here I'd thought Robert Earle and Shirley had brought those flowers to soften up Gladys. They must have picked them up at my door and pocketed the card.

"I'm sorry," I fibbed with great aplomb. "I've been too busy to remember my manners. Yes. I got them and they were beautiful."

"Just wanted to be sure," he said, arranging his chair to face me more directly. "A little something to say I enjoyed being with you. So what's on for this weekend?"

I withdrew my hand because at that moment I knew, regardless of how much fun I was having, a little space between us was needed — at least until I got Gladys's project under wraps. It was probably just that uncomfortable feeling I get when I've got too much on my plate; nevertheless, this wasn't fair to either one of us.

"My son is visiting," I said. "He'll be staying at Bud's place, Seahaven. I want to spend some time with him."

"Oh." In the dim light, I couldn't quite read his expression.

"There's always next weekend, though," I said as I gathered my things and headed for the door. "I'll give you a ring later."

Silky darkness enveloped the Jeep as I navigated the beach roads back to the Morning Glory Inn, calming me and allowing me to muster my thoughts and prepare for tomorrow. Then technology intruded. My cell rang. It was William.

"Hi, Mom. Listen, Joe's dad needs to leave tomorrow . . . early. In fact, I'll be at that little airport around eight thirty in the morning. Is that doable for you?"

"No problem, I'll be there."

Perfect. Will's slightly early arrival could be just what I needed to speed things up a bit. I'd call Wink in the morning and let him know it would be after lunch before I could get to the site.

Wednesday morning, after catching up on Will's latest news, I watched him finish up a second helping of scrambled eggs at a diner and said, "By the way, did you ever find any information on that company I asked you to look into, I.T.N.F. TestCo Group?"

"No, and I've made a pretty thorough search. But I'll keep looking."

"Atta boy. If anyone can find it, you can."

Later, on the drive to Seahaven we had a lengthy discussion on the presentation and I brought him up to speed on the new deadline the bankers had given me. We arrived at the beach house a little before lunch. Gladys met us at the parking area by the road with Tulip.

"Can I take Tulip out on the beach?" Will asked after I introduced him to Gladys.

Tulip stopped in her tracks and swung her head in my direction. I swear that hound can understand English.

"Sure," I said.

"I've got cold cuts, chicken, and potato salad in the fridge whenever you're ready for lunch," Gladys said.

"Will, did you hear Gladys?"

"Gotcha!" Will yelled as he banged up the stairs and headed for the house, Tulip racing ahead of him.

I turned my attention back to Gladys as we walked to the house. It had only been a few days, but I hardly recognized her. Her facial features were relaxed, her short grey hair, previously worn in tight curls, now blew freely about her face. Her jeans were rolled up to her knees and she was barefooted. Quite a change from leather tie-ups and elastic-waisted polyester pants.

She looked so happy I decided not to tell her what the sheriff had said about Robert Earle and the grill cover. Besides, who knew, it was still an open investigation and anything could happen. Anyway, the sheriff did say he wanted to talk to her. I'd let him tell her.

Later, after we finished our lunch on the gazebo, Will took off with Tulip again and Gladys and I chatted as we cleaned up. "Your Bud sure is a nice man," Gladys said.

Now that was news. "Pardon," I said. "You've met him?"

"Why yes. He and I enjoyed iced tea and a long conversation the other day when he dropped by to make sure some building materials he'd ordered had been delivered. I believe he said he'd be replacing all the porch railings."

Something that should have been done years ago. It's a wonder someone hadn't fallen through one of them. A delicious image of Bud's girlfriend flailing helplessly as she plummeted to the ground came to mind. I smiled inwardly but then realized Gladys was looking at me expectantly. "I'm sorry. What did you say?"

"I said I can't believe you let such a great

guy get away."

"First of all, Gladys, I didn't let Bud get away. I . . . oh, you know what?" I said, deciding this was yet another conversation best deferred. No way I wanted to get between their new friendship or try to explain my old marriage. Not with all I had to do. "You're right. He's definitely a nice-looking man and he'll make someone a nice husband someday."

Will bounded back up the stairs from the beach. "Remember, Mom, I'm taking Gladys for a boat ride tomorrow," he said as he flew past us and into the house. Henri kept a twenty-two-foot, flat-bottom skiff in a slip at Captain Eddie's, the marina right across the road on the sound side. "But don't worry, I'll have your presentation ready before Tuesday. I'm going to work on it Saturday and Sunday. Get everything set up so all I need is the data to plug in . . . no later than Monday."

I looked at my watch. "Speaking of that," I said. "I need to go. I've got to get back to work."

SEVENTEEN

When I arrived on Gladys's property, I left
the Jeep in my usual spot under some trees
at the edge of the field so I wouldn't beat it
up further driving to the rig on a dozer trail.
I could barely hear the rig through the
woods, but what I heard made me stop and
listen closer. The sounds coming from the
drill site were slightly different, almost like
an echo. Good grief. If this was more
trouble, I needed some water. I opened the
door to the backseat and plundered through
the stuff on the floor for an unopened bottle
of Evian I knew was back there somewhere.

Ahh, there it was, wedged under the seat-
adjustment bar on the passenger side. When
I straightened up to get in better position to
make the reach, I spotted something poking
out from under a folded beach towel I keep
on the backseat in case Tulip takes an
unscheduled swim. I lifted the towel. Will's
laptop. Damn. It must have slid there dur-

ing our trip from the airport. I bent again to reach for the water wondering when I'd have time to take it back to him.

I was still butt up, face to the floorboard, reaching under the seat, when I felt a tap on my back. My friend the rattler must have been lurking somewhere in my brain cells because I nearly jerked my arm out of the socket trying to back out of the car. And thus I tangled legs with and knocked over the person who had tapped me.

"What the fuck!" said an irate Shirley Walton from where she sat in the hay stubble.

"What the fuck, yourself," I said from where I also was sprawled on the ground. "You scared the hell out of me. What do you want?"

"I want my mother," she said, her face in major pout mode.

"We all do. Mine's dead, and yours will get in touch with you in her own time, not yours."

Shirley stood up and brushed wisps of hay from her shorts. "You don't understand. There's a bunch of detectives from the sheriff's department at my house right now, tearing the place apart looking for . . . what? I don't know."

I stood up and brushed myself off. "Did you ask if they had a search warrant?"

182

"Of course I did. You think I'm stupid?"

Resist the temptation, Cleo. "Actually, Shirley, I think you're probably not stupid. In fact, I think you're smart, smart enough to know your mother is neither crazy nor incapacitated in any way. Moreover" — I took her elbow, and walked her toward her white Lexus — "if you'll stop and think about all these things that are happening to you-your cousin murdered, your mother taking leave of you and your brother, the police questioning you, your house being searched — you'd realize all these things are happening for a reason. Either you're part of the reason, or else you know things. Things that in the deepest recesses of your heart would lead you to what that reason is."

I opened the car door for her.

Shirley got in but didn't say anything, just sat there.

"Maybe you need to do some soul searching," I said. "Because I can tell you from experience, once your mother is really gone, as in dead, no amount of reasoning can bring her back."

"Dead? Who said anything about dead?"

"I'm just saying . . . all these high-pressure tactics you and Robert Earle are employing could have unintended consequences." I looked past her to the interior of the car. On the passenger seat, poking halfway out of a plastic shopping bag, was one of several packages of cigarillos. Shirley made an exasperated little huffing noise and started the engine.

"By the way," I said as she pulled the car into gear, "how do you guys always know when I arrive on site?"

"Any fool can see you when you pass by the house on the way here."

"See," I said, patting the door frame, "you are smart. You should've been a detective." Shirley rolled her eyes, sniffed, and roared off.

Cigarillos. Did she buy them for herself or someone else? I wasn't sure, but I thought I even detected a faint odor on her. The same odor I'd smelled on the back porch of the old tenant house behind the well. On the very day I'd fallen into that well and someone had maybe even helped me over the edge.

Interesting.

The difference in the sound emanating from the drill site became clear as soon as I broke from the woods into the clearing where the crew was working. Not an echo after all; two drills were grinding away at my underground mountain . . . and my dwindling bank account.

"Wink," I said, pointing to the other rig, "where did that come from?"

He looked to the far side of the clearing where a second crew loaded augers flights and prepared to move to another hole. "Well, look, we need to hustle to make your deadline. We were doing pretty good too, until the chain on the kelly broke on that piece-of-shit backup rig. Then I had to call Purdue's. Lucky for us, they'd finished the engine work on the rig you and the boys dumped in the creek —"

"Oh now, wait a minute . . ."

He grinned. "Door's just wired shut on the driver's side, but that won't stop us from drilling holes, so I sent Mule to pick it up and called in another crew to run it. While he was gone, Stick and I actually fixed the kelly on the backup. Now we're operating two crews. It's all good news, since it means we'll be done here Friday."

"See, Wink, that's why you get the big bucks. I'm just glad I was taking my son to his dad's and missed all the extra drama. I'd have had a stroke."

By quitting time, I'd caught up with entering all the new drill results in my records and on my map. In the morning I'd start the tedious job of logging the core samples.

Back at the Morning Glory I nibbled halfheartedly at a Subway ham on wheat, but the heat and stress had left me with little appetite. I switched on the TV, then turned it off, irritated by the clamoring herd of anchormen and women and their glow-in-the-dark teeth. It seemed a better plan to break open my newest James Hall novel — I loved to read about Florida — pour myself a Jack Black on ice, then hit the hay.

Then I remembered Will's laptop

I got up and retrieved my cell.

"Your laptop is in my Jeep. Slid under some stuff in the backseat."

"Oh, man. I haven't missed it yet. You want me to come get it? I could use Dad's truck."

"Is he there?"

"No. But he's coming tomorrow to cook Gladys and me a frogmore stew. She's never had one. You want me to tell him you'll be here to help eat it?"

I could hear the hope in his voice but I was used to squashing it, so I said, "No. I don't have time. But thanks for asking. I'll just drop the computer off and head back here. I need to be on-site all day Saturday to see that the job's wrapped up nice and

186

tidy. I may even have to work Sunday too."

"Okay," he said sulkily. "But I wish I could talk you into . . ."

I cut him off. "Gotta go, sugar. I'll leave all the data you need on the kitchen counter with the laptop. We'll talk later."

I clicked off, flopped face first onto the chenille bedspread, and breathed in the fragrance of lavender-scented detergent. Next thing I knew, the traffic report for the greater Jacksonville area blared out from the room's radio alarm clock. It was six a.m.

My luck held all day Thursday — no earthquakes or hurricanes or suicide bombers — so I left everything in Wink's capable hands and knocked off a little early. I reached the Causeway Bridge to Wrightsville Beach just as the sun began its westward slide into Bogue Sound.

Grabbing Will's computer, I started the long trek from the parking area down the boardwalk that led to the house. I slowed a bit to savor the sea breeze on my face, the muffled sound of thundering waves, the crying of gulls and shorebirds working the beach. Maybe it was the angle of the late afternoon sunlight, but Seahaven seemed to shimmer in the golden light, a mirage that could disappear in an instant, which was the antithesis of how I'd always felt about it. In my mind, Seahaven was one of those houses that would always be there. Through hurricanes and zoning changes and generations, it would last.

I trotted up the steep wooden exterior steps at the side of the house that lead to the kitchen door. As I stepped in and set the laptop on the counter, I noticed a sliding-glass door that led to the front deck was open, a gauzy curtain blowing pleasantly in the breeze. "Anybody home?" I crossed the great room and slid the door closed. The house grew even quieter. I called out again. "Gladys? You here?" Then I heard it. A sound like someone had dropped something on the hardwood floor overhead — something small, like a pencil. "Will?" I headed for the stairs.

I went up and poked my head into his bedroom. Unmade bed, wet bathing suit on the floor in the adjoining bathroom. Like the great room below, the upstairs bedrooms on the ocean side all had glass doors that opened onto a deck running the complete width of the house, though the upper floor, and thus the deck, was cantilevered out an additional five feet. I stepped out on the deck, looked up and down the beach. Just a few late afternoon surfers. No Will.

188

I walked up the hall to the room I'd given Gladys only a few days ago. Here, everything was neat as a pin, the bed made, towels in the bathroom folded. A pang of anxiety made me walk to the closet to see if her suitcase was gone.

I opened the door, and that's when a large man in a black ski mask surged out of the closet, knocking me down. I guess being flat on my back wasn't conducive to rational thought because, like an idiot, I grabbed his sneakered foot and tripped him. Maybe it was just the instinct to protect what's mine — or used to be mine. In any event, he went down like a felled tree.

"Umph!"

Don't ask me what, but there was something suspiciously familiar about the man now scrambling to regain his footing.

"Robert Earle?" I said as I grabbed for the ski mask.

He dodged my hand, bounced to his feet, and jerked me to mine by my ponytail.

"Ouch! Stop that, you moron!" I kicked out with and caught him square on the shin with my field boot.

It was as if I'd poured lighter fluid on a charcoal fire. He bellowed, reached out with one hand and grabbed me by my neck with an intensity that told me he meant to kill

189

me right then and there. With his other hand, he grabbed the waist of my jeans and lifted me off the floor. It didn't take me long to realize he was planning to use my head like a battering ram and smash it into the sliding glass doors. I threw my hands up just in time to protect my face. My arms, shoulder and the right side of my forehead took the brunt of the blow. He was grabbing me everywhere, hellbent on trying to swing me headfirst into that glass door.

But he wasn't getting it done because I was kicking, biting, and scratching — anything to get out of his clutches. Finally, I managed to connect a knee with his crotch. Air whooshed from his lungs as he dropped me and staggered backwards. That gave me the second I needed to get out onto the deck.

I tried to hold the door closed. With ten times my strength, he rammed it open so hard, it all but busted from the track. Then, his fingers flexed like eagle talons, he began to stalk toward me. For every step he took forward, I backed up one, trying desperately to think of a way to escape this maniac. Suddenly, I felt the railing at my back. Trapped like a rat! I could always jump. Hell, no. The drop to the ground was twenty-five feet straight into a rock garden.

Before I had time to come up with a plan, the asshole charged me again. I dropped to my knees and shot between his feet like a rabbit. He lunged right over my head and into the railing.

Good old Bud and his knack for procrastination. With the sound of splintering wood, my attacker sailed right through the rotted railing and into the open air beyond.

My legs were too wobbly to stand, so I crawled to the edge of the deck. Then a creepy thought hit me. What if he wasn't down there? What if he'd somehow landed on the deck below and was coming back up after me right now?

I leaned over the edge and peered down. Lucky break. The ski-masked Robert Earle was lying facedown in a group planting of yucca trees. And they don't call the long, spike-tipped leaves Spanish bayonets for nothing.

I watched the prone figure for a moment. It didn't move. I pulled out my cell, incredibly not broken. I told Bud when he answered to drop everything and get the hell over to Seahaven.

EIGHTEEN

I was outside directing the Wrightsville Beach police to where the body lay when Bud stormed onto the scene. To his credit, he stood by quietly while I explained to the cops what had happened.

"I felt his jugular for a pulse," I told them. "Other than that, I haven't touched him."

In five minutes, a crew of paramedics and first responders — firemen — arrived carrying a stretcher and lots of noisy two-way radios. As they took over the scene, Bud and I retreated to a grouping of wicker furniture situated on the ground floor patio under the deck and perched on the edge of the sofa.

"What the hell's going on, Cleo? One minute I'm at Lowe's getting some stuff I need to fix the railings and next thing, I'm getting a panicked call from you."

"Well, let me start by saying you're a little late on the railings." I gave Bud a quick sketch of what happened.

"He had on a ski mask?" Bud asked incredulously. "Good god! He was a robber or —"

"No. I don't think he was a robber," I interrupted.

"What then?"

"I think the man in the mask is Robert Earle Walton."

"Who?"

"Gladys Walton's son."

"Why on earth would Gladys's son want to kill you? For that matter, how would he know where you were? None of this makes any sense . . ." Bud said. "Start over. Tell me exactly what happened."

"Actually," said one of the city cops, overhearing him. "There'll be a couple of detectives here shortly to ask you some questions. Why don't you wait until they get here? That way, you won't have to tell your story so many times."

Bud stood up impatiently blowing out a long breath and stepped into the guest quarters under the house. When he returned, he handed me a water and sat with his arm over my shoulder. In my world — a man's world that few women inhabit — strong men are generally a nuisance; indeed, they're often obstacles in my way, but sometimes . . . well, a good one can be a comfort.

"I'd hoped Will and Gladys would be back from their boat trip by now," I said.

"You know how Will is. He gets out on the water and loses all track of time —"

"I don't want Gladys to see her son like this," I said.

"Oh my God," he said, almost under his breath.

"What?"

"That's my ski mask!"

I glanced quickly at the body again. "God, you're right. I remember it from our Vail trip." I thought for a minute. Things formally murky began to coalesce and gain some clarity. "It's all starting to make sense now."

"What?"

"He came here hoping to find Gladys, got surprised by me instead, so he hid in the closet. When it looked like I was going to find him, he must have seen the mask and decided to make me think I'd interrupted a robbery or something. His plan was probably just to scare the life out of me, then make a getaway and hope the whole thing blew over. Might have worked too, if I hadn't tripped him"

"You what?"

"I know, I should have let him hightail it out of the house, but I didn't," I sighed. "When I called him by name and kicked him in the shin, I guess he panicked. At any rate, from there, he flew into a rage."

Bud patted my shoulders and gave me a reassuring hug.

"They're here," said one of the city cops, pointing to two detectives in khakis and shades. One was older, tall with an ex-Marine look to him. The other was about thirty and had slicked-back, dark curly hair raked behind his ears, *à la* Antonio Banderas.

They removed their sports jackets, pulled on latex gloves, and began their inspection of the scene. When they seemed satisfied that enough photos had been taken, they rolled the body in the yucca plants onto its back.

I thought I saw them both flinch. I stepped over for a closer look of the body right-side up. I saw what had made them flinch.

A yucca spike was sticking through the ski mask into an eye socket and had to be poking at least four inches into Robert Earle's brain. Bud, who'd come up behind me, saw what I saw; he turned my face to his chest and held me tight.

The older detective had to pull out the

yucca spike before he could remove the mask. When this was accomplished, he said, "You can look now, Miss Cooper. Is that the man you say it is?"

"Yes," I said and moved back to the couch where I gulped a slug of water.

"Damn," Bud said, "I can't believe this. Someone killed in my home."

Tears burned behind my eyes, and I nodded in agreement then looked up to see the detectives heading my way.

Detective Terry, the older one, and the younger Saunders had a lot of questions. They were not real happy or satisfied with the facts, primarily that after a scuffle with me, my ex-husband's house-guest's son had ended up dead. I pointed out that a headlong dive through rotted railing followed by a 25-foot fall and a yucca spike through the brain was what killed him, not me. The ski mask did work in my favor, though, as it pretty much proved the guy was not there for a social visit. Still, they were perplexed about the mask, so I told them it was actually Bud's ski mask and gave them a skeleton of an explanation as to why Robert Earle wanted to see his mother and why she was hiding from him.

Detective Terry, who had the most remarkable eyes, intense gray and like laser-beams, listened intently, then said, "I can buy that Mr. Walton put on the ski mask to make you think he was just an intruder, but suffice it to say, you'd probably benefit if Mr. Walton was permanently kept away from his mother." I felt Bud stiffen at my side. I pushed away from the back of the sofa, sat up straight and said, "It wouldn't have made a difference to me one way or another. I have an iron-clad legal contract with Mrs. Walton. She made it clear to me that she didn't want to see him. I was just accommodating her."

The two detectives huddled a moment, then Saunders said, "So, just for the record, you think Mr. Walton was just trying to scare you, not actually kill you, and that basically this was just an accident?"

"I think so," I said.

"Only he knows the answer to that, and he isn't talking anymore" Bud added.

"You gentlemen might want to have a talk with Sheriff Evans over in Onslow County, the Waltons' home county. He has information I'm sure you'd be interested in. I'd like to go into more detail myself, but right now, I'm concerned about my son and Mrs. Walton not being here and would like to go find them."

Terry turned the laser beams on me again, then said, "I need contact numbers for both of you."

The mob finally pulled out almost two hours later, including the ambulance carrying Robert Earle's remains. Bud and I went upstairs to the kitchen. "I've got to get word to Sheriff Evans about Robert Earle, let him know to expect a call from those two detectives. Then I have to go look for Gladys and Will. They've been gone far too long."

Bud was leaning over the sink, looking out the window past the expanse of dunes to the marina across the street. "Huh. Some of those policemen stopped in at Captain Eddie's — getting drinks, I guess — and I think those detectives are with them. At least that black sedan looks like a detective car."

I moved beside him and peered out just in time to see Will come out the marina door.

"Oh, thank goodness," I said, turning from the sink. "At least Will and Gladys are back from their boat trip."

Bud headed for the liquor cabinet. "I'll fix up some drinks. I know I could use one."

He was adding a lime twist to Gladys's Grey Goose and tonic when Will burst into the room, "Are you guys alright? The police said there was an accident over here, that Gladys's son fell through a railing. What the hell?"

"Yes, we're fine," I said as I pulled the door back open and looked down the stairs to the grounds below. "Where's Gladys?"

"She took your Jeep and left," Will said, opening the fridge.

Bud and I stared at his protruding backside. Then, said in unison, "Left?"

Will's head popped up. "Yeah. Gladys and I were heading over here — cutting through the tackle shop at Eddie's — when, out the front window, we saw an ambulance and a bunch of cop cars leaving the house. We panicked," he said, his eyes still wide as he cracked open a Bud Light. "But before we could make it to the front door, a couple of policemen came in. Gladys hustled over and asked them what was going on. That's when these two guys — they said they were detectives — asked us who we were, then told us what happened. I can't believe it!"

"Take it easy," I said. "You're going to hyperventilate."

Will took a gulp of beer. "I could tell Gladys was really shocked. I mean, I was so shocked, I couldn't speak. Then, all the sudden Gladys got real calm. She asked the detectives where they were taking her son, then told me to tell you she was borrowing the Jeep. The keys were already in it. She jumped in and took off after the ambulance so fast there wasn't much I could do, but I figured it was okay, it being her son and all . . ."

I slammed my hand on the kitchen counter. "Jesus H. Christ, Will! What in the hell were you thinking?"

"What do you mean?" Will asked aghast.

"Seriously, son, you really have to start using your head for something besides a beer funnel! The woman's in shock, for God's sake. She's just lost her firstborn child and you let her drive off all by herself?"

"Stop yelling at him," Bud said. "I'd have done the same thing. What was he supposed to do? Try and tell a grown woman what to do? Good luck with that!"

Lord, deliver me from a world of boorish men.

"She seemed fine to me, Mom. And I did give her a hug. Oh, Yeah — that's when she told me to tell you she'd leave your Jeep at the Morning Glory Inn."

"Why didn't you say that in the first place?" At least I knew now where she would go after she followed Robert Earle's body. I looked at Bud expectantly.

"Yes," he said, "I'll take you there, but

first, chill out before you pop a bolt. Besides, you need to eat something. We all do. It's too late to mess with frogmore stew. I'll cook some burgers on the grill."

I agreed to wait awhile but called the Morning Glory several times during dinner and got no answer. Finally, after we finished eating, I connected with Betsy, the innkeeper, and asked if she had checked in a nice older woman named Gladys Walton this evening.

"No, I didn't check her in," Betsy said. "But she did drop off your Jeep. I told her to put it in the garden parking lot just below your room. She asked me to call her a cab and I did."

Rats! "Did she say where she was going?"

"Sorry, she didn't."

I clicked off, found the card with the sheriff's cell number on it, and called him. I was sent straight to his voicemail. I left him a message to expect a call from Wrightsville Beach detectives regarding Robert Earle Walton and asked him to call me back.

I was barely aware of what Bud was saying on the way to the Morning Glory Inn. Snippets of his dialogue, like an uninteresting book on tape, played just outside my conscious thought. Then a pause in the tape caused me to turn and face him. "Uh, sorry?"

He frowned. "Relax. Everything's going to be fine. You'll see. Gladys will call you when she's ready. You're going to bring your project in and before you know it, you'll be rich and all this will be behind you."

"I guess," I mumbled.

Despite my best efforts to keep my business with Gladys and the project a simple, uncomplicated option to test and purchase from day one, one force had acted against me: unmitigated greed in the form of the Walton siblings. Did Robert Earle's death prove my instincts had been correct? What would the sheriff say when he found out about Robert Earle? Was Shirley involved? Was the whole project dead?

Like a compulsive gambler I told myself to keep playing. *Don't fold yet, girl. Just hold on until the last of the test results come in and the bank grants the loan.* Then I'd pay Gladys. The land and mining rights would be mine and any and all reasons for this chaos would be gone, just like Bud said. Right?

I looked at Bud, driving and still talking. I smiled as if I were paying attention and worried about Gladys. Wherever she was, she was probably wishing she'd never agreed to stay at Seahaven. Now, because of me, there would always be a stigma attached to Seahaven. Someone had been killed there. Gloom and depression settled over me with the weight of a lead x-ray vest.

I laid my hand on Bud's arm. "You know, I wish I could turn back time. I wish I had hid Gladys somewhere else. I wish . . . a thousand things . . ."

Now Bud had nothing to say.

"I hope you'll accept my apology for bringing such a nightmare to Seahaven. And that, over time, you can forget all the horror that happened there today."

He sighed. "We need to get something straight, Cleo. It's me who owes you an apology. Not the other way around. This whole mess is, in fact, my fault."

"How in the hell do you figure that?"

"Because if I'd listened to you in the first place, if I hadn't blown you off that night over at your house right after you found that body, none of this would have happened. You told me then you thought Gladys's kids could be a danger to her. I thought you were overreacting and well, I was way too busy trying to get into your pants that night to take anything you said seriously."

"Thanks for trying to make me feel better, but I know whose fault —" I stopped. I could feel my voice getting all shaky. I hate when that happens. Fortunately, Sheriff Evans returned my call just at that time.

"Could've been worse," the sheriff said at the news about Robert Earle.

"How's that?" I asked.

"Could've been you with a Spanish bayonet through your brain."

"I see your point. Um, no pun intended."

"Where's Gladys now?" the sheriff asked brusquely.

"I'm not exactly sure but I would think she went wherever the ambulance took Robert Earle. I do know she dropped my car at the Morning Glory and took a cab from there."

"Well, we were both right to be concerned about what might become of Gladys Walton at the hands of her own children. The Wrightsville Beach police found a clincher piece of evidence."

"What was that?"

"The Power of Attorney you've been telling me about. It was folded in half and stuffed in Robert Earle's waistband under his shirt, all ready for Gladys's signature."

"Well," I said. "That's that, then." I felt something, but I don't think it was relief.

"It is for me. Especially when you combine it with the gun we found in his room, the one that killed Irene. Plus, his actions since you started testing his mother's property and his motive . . . well, it makes a very solid case that he killed his aunt. For all we know, if Gladys had refused to sign his Power of Attorney, he might have killed her too. It's not like he didn't try already."

Gun? He never told me about the gun. That was pretty incriminating. "Can you tell me exactly where you found the gun in his room?"

"I don't guess it matters now, since for all intents and purposes, the case will be closed. We found it in his sock drawer."

"Oh. One other thing, Sheriff. Does Robert Earle smoke cigarillos?"

"I don't know. Why do you ask? Wait — did *you* find cigarillo butts somewhere?" the sheriff asked, annoyed.

"Actually, uh, I did come across them, near the well where Irene's body was dumped. Does that make you wonder if someone else was involved? If I still should be worried?"

"No. We know about it. I'd say it's probably a totally unrelated matter. Probably one of the farm workers, a migrant just passing through. I don't think you or Gladys have anything to worry about anymore."

"Thanks, Sheriff," I said and clicked off.

It had occurred to me to mention the cigarillos on Shirley's front seat, but I didn't. Maybe I would, after my project was safely under wraps.

First thing in the morning, I'd find Gladys. Then I'd feel better.

NINETEEN

Looking for Gladys in her own home seemed the logical place to start. A simple telephone call to the house would have been easier, but I knew I'd get a runaround if Shirley answered. Maybe I'd get lucky and Gladys would be alone, the dutiful daughter wouldn't be there.

The first thing I noticed Friday morning when I pulled up in the driveway was the absence of a wreath on her door. Funeral wreaths are a big tradition in the South, especially in small towns and rural areas that receive weekly instead of daily papers. Ivan Thorpe's pickup was parked behind Shirley's white Lexus, and Gladys's car was in its usual spot. Well, it was early yet for neighbors to stop by. I lowered all my car windows to half-mast for Tulip, got out, and went up the porch stairs.

Shirley opened the door to my knock, and waved me in without saying a word. She was still in her Victoria's Secret pajamas. (Again, my superior powers of deduction, combined with the huge VS on the front of the soft gray jersey set, let me know the brand name in a snap.)

"Hi," she said glumly.

"Hi."

"I'm making coffee. Want some?"

"Sure."

I sat at the table where I'd spent many mornings chatting with Gladys and now watched her daughter as she busied herself with the mindless task. After what I felt was a polite interval, I said, "Sorry about Robert Earle . . . I think he had a lot of issues . . ."

Shirley didn't answer, just kept spooning grounds into the filter on the coffee maker. I didn't think she was going to say anything. Then, with no warning, she turned on me so abruptly that she hit the filter tray, sending a spray of hazelnut grounds across the counter. "This is all your fault! My brother's dead because of you!"

I decided to drop any attempt at ceremony.

"Me? He was trying to kill me when he fell, Shirley. I interrupted him as he was lying in wait for your mother so he could make her sign your damn Power of Attorney. Doesn't that mean anything to you? Don't you feel any responsibility here?"

"Of course not. It was you who drove us to do what we did. We had to make sure our mother didn't cheat us. You just wait. I'm going to talk some more to those detectives in Wrightsville, and when I do, I'll convince them that you should be charged with murder."

"Good luck with that!" I said, not feeling in the least as confident as I sounded.

"Yeah, Shirley's right," said Ivan, who had creepily materialized in the kitchen. "An investigation will prove that you got rid of Robert Earle because he could prove that you were taking advantage of Gladys."

I stood up from the table. "I'm not discussing this any further. Actually, I'm here to see your mom. Where is she?"

Shirley gave me a glare that would have flash-frozen a fried turkey and said, "You know full well she's not here."

Now it was my turn to act outraged. "Not here? Cut the crap."

"You cut the crap," Ivan shot back. "You're the one who's known all along where she is. Not us." Then, directing his words to Shirley, he pointed at me and said, "Don't let her tell you she doesn't know where your mom is because she does. She's got her hidden somewhere and she's playing dumb to confuse us."

Suddenly Shirley's emotional state changed again. This time to vulnerable and scared.

"Hush, Ivan," Shirley pleaded. "I don't know what to think. Anyway, this isn't the time. My brother is dead and I don't know what to do. What kind of arrangements to make. I don't know how to do any of this stuff. I need my mother to take care of everything. Like she always has." She dropped her head in her hands and began to cry.

Ivan softened. "Now, now, baby. Don't you worry. I'm here to help you. I'll always be here, unlike your crazy mother. You never could count on her. You know that."

Good grief. I'd seen this type of manipulation before. Bad guy sweeps rich, naive girl off her feet, gains her trust, takes her money. Granted, most of my experience with such a scenario was from late night movies, but I could spot a pro when I saw one.

Then an alarm bell went off in the part of my brain that spots trouble. The faint but unmistakable sweet smell enveloping Ivan triggered it.

Cigarillos.

You know how it is in the early morning

when fog lifts from a pasture at the edge of some woods, and you can start to make out the individual trees? Well, that was how I felt watching Ivan hold Shirley. The mist had lifted to reveal what was actually there. He was up to something, and it wasn't just sweet talk.

Shirley's crying got a little softer. I was just turning to leave when she said, "Today should be one of the happiest of my life. I should be sharing my new marriage with Mom. Instead I'm dealing with death."

Better to deal with it than experience it, I was thinking before her words sunk in. "What? New marriage?"

Her face brightened briefly. "Ivan and I got married yesterday afternoon at the courthouse. Now he can help me all the time. Apparently, I need it." Then Shirley's face collapsed again and she blubbered, "Can you imagine? All my wedding anniversaries will also be the anniversary of my brother's death."

I'd be willing to bet ruining all his sister's future anniversaries wasn't a goal Robert Earle had ever set himself.

"Now, baby," Ivan said with a fierce glance in my direction, "you're just overwhelmed right now — through no fault of your own. But I'm here and I'll make it all better."

"I'll let myself out," I said, readying myself to leave. If his gaze had been real steel daggers, I wouldn't have made it out the door.

TWENTY

Parking in my usual spot in the dappled shade at the edge of the woods, I felt more relief to be finishing a job than I had ever felt in my career. Today was the last day of initial testing for this project, the light at the end of the tunnel was getting brighter and it seemed now that maybe that light wasn't a train barreling down on me after all. Maybe. My head already ached from my encounter with the newlyweds, Mr. and Mrs. Thorpe. Rubbing my temple I opened the door for Tulip. She crossed the hay field and disappeared into the woods as I followed at a more sedate pace.

As soon as I stepped under the green canopy of pines and hardwoods, the faraway, reassuring throb of two diesel engines at my site acted like balm to my ragged nerve endings.

I had so many questions, and they all seemed to go back to that first day when someone had watched me at the well where I found Irene's body — someone who knew it was there.

Someone smoking cigarillos.

It worked to my advantage that the sheriff believed Robert Earle to be Irene's killer; no danger of him shutting down my site for my protection. But was it Robert Earle?

I was no detective and the sheriff didn't need me to solve — or in this case, upset — his case for Irene Mizzell's murder. On the other hand, it would be a handy bit of information to know if the real killer was still out there. Especially if his motive was ultimately to gain control of my granite rock deposit.

I had a theory. True, it was all jumbled up right now, but I only needed to untangle it.

Admittedly, some parts of my theory required a rubber imagination and several very big *ifs*. The first big one — if Ivan were to marry Shirley — had now been realized. That led quite naturally to the second: what if something happened to Gladys? Like she turned up dead or committed or in a retirement home? If Shirley convinced her to sign a Power of Attorney, then Ivan would be in a perfect position to take control of everything since he was obviously well on his way to controlling Shirley.

If only I knew what really had happened to Irene. It seemed I should begin with the premise she'd been shot by mistake by someone who thought she was Gladys. She'd been targeted from behind in Gladys's kitchen in the early evening while the kids were eating out. Yet Robert Earle could have doubled back and shot Irene, believing her to be his mom. He wouldn't have known about Gladys's trip since her whole purpose was to get away from him and Shirley.

However, I'd never seen any evidence that he smoked cigarillos and I knew Ivan did. Ivan also struck me as the more logical choice because he'd been in town that day. He'd even told me he'd seen Gladys and Irene together around noon.

No matter how I looked at it, I kept coming back to the fact that with Robert Earle dead, Gladys committed or without power over her affairs, and Shirley completely under his sway, Ivan could conceivably control all the family money.

Okay, there was the matter of the gun found in Robert Earle's sock drawer. But Ivan had continual access to the house and could easily have planted it there. In my mind, the plan the Walton darlings had hatched to take over their mother's affairs probably started out to do only that. But once Ivan entered the picture, it turned into a scheme to take control of everything.

All he had to do was encourage two spoiled brats to get a little more gung-ho in going after what they wanted. That made sense. More sense than a son trying to kill his mother.

Of course, no theory is perfect.

For instance, there was still a big unanswered question: if Ivan had sent Robert Earle to Seahaven — while he and Shirley were conveniently getting hitched — how did he know where Gladys was?

I didn't have a chance to come up with an answer because Tulip shot out of the woods behind me and ran to the clearing ahead, where she greeted Wink with an excited bark. "Hey, purdy girl," said Wink as he pulled Tulip's silky ears and patted her muscular sides.

"Wink," I said, "what's happening?"

He handed me a hard hat and said, "I'm about to knock heads is what's happening." He glared at the sheepish drill crew. Mule and Stick ducked their heads and watched the mud oozing up from the core hole. The last core was being brought into the light of day for the first time since it had cooled from a molten mass some one thousand million years ago.

"What's going on?"

"I don't know how many times I'm going to have to spell it out to those boys: don't leave your truck unlocked."

"Unlocked?"

I glared at Mule and Stick through squinted lids, then, realizing they wouldn't be able to detect my full scowl behind my sunglasses, lifted them so they could get the full effect.

"Tool box is locked, man!" Mule yelled over the thrumming, grinding sounds of the diesel. "And Wink has all the data and cores locked in his truck."

"Yeah!" Stick shouted.

"Don't matter, you idiots!" Wink shouted back. "Long as each of you got a spare key to my truck hidden in your glove box, someone could find it if they really wanted to."

"Now that's really paranoid, man. Maybe you need to see a shrink," Mule shouted back at Wink. Then he shook his head and turned his attention back to his drilling.

"When did you notice this?"

"This morning's the first time. I just checked his as I walked by it over yonder," Wink said, indicating Mule's truck. "I asked him when was the last time he thought to lock it up and he says, 'Out here in the woods, man?' "

"So they probably haven't locked up since we've been on this job?"

"Probably not."

"What about the other team?"

Wink shook his head in the negative.

I gave a Marge Simpson growl.

"No harm's done," Wink said. "Nothing's missing. But you never know. We already had trouble with that guy — what's his name . . . Robert Earle?"

"*Was* his name. He's now the late Robert Earle," I corrected. "Start hauling out those last few boxes of cores. While I log them, I'll bring you up to date on the continuing drama with the Walton clan."

After I told Wink the news, we both fell into a troubled silence as we worked. I sat on the tailgate while Wink cracked open box after box of cores in the order in which they'd come from the ground.

I didn't know about him, but I did some of my best thinking while immersed in a mindless task. Logging cores of granite was fairly rote because the mineralogy changed very little throughout the deposit. Using standard geologic shorthand, my granite was a granite gneiss, or Ggn, and had widely spaced joints filled with milky quartz, or

Qz. With each box containing nine feet of core, and most of the cores taken to a depth of at least one hundred feet, well, you see the need for the geologic shorthand.

The morning ground into a hot muggy afternoon. I kept logging, on and on, swatting mosquitoes and mopping sweat. The throbbing and grinding of the drill literally vibrated the bed of the pickup. Diesel fumes enveloped me, disturbed only when a rare breeze stirred the humid air. I was in heaven.

Lunchtime came. Wink, the four drillers, and I had our last lunch together as a team then trooped back through the woods to wrap up the job.

Wink and I fell back into our routine, him cracking open the boxes, me entering them on the log sheet, making notations about weathering, jointing, and any other distinguishing characteristics, when suddenly I stopped dead, mid-log.

"Oh, shit," I said.

"What's the matter?" Wink demanded. "You okay?"

I blinked, turned to him. "I just thought of something and I sure hope it's not true."

"What?"

"Remember I told you Robert Earle tried to make me believe he had another company — one out of Charlotte operating under

I.T.N.F. TestCo Group — that offered him an option better than the one I gave Gladys?"

"Yeah. But you said he didn't have a Power of Attorney signed by Gladys, so it wasn't worth squat."

"Yes, but it would result in a huge legal battle and we all know court cases are a crapshoot at best."

"True . . ." Wink paused. "Dang girl, you're pale as a sheet. Let me get you some water . . ."

I held up my hand. "I'll be okay. Hear me out . . ." I paused and took a deep breath. "Wink? What if I-T-N-F stands for Ivan Thorpe and Nash Finley?"

Wink gave me an uncomprehending look.

I tried to explain. "Just like V-S stands for Victoria's Secret, and G-g-n stands for granite gneiss."

"I know what an acronym is, and I know who Nash Finley is. Know he's slicker than a puppy's peter and twice as nasty, but who's Ivan Thorpe?"

"Wait. Back the trolley up," I said. "Why did you say Nash is slick and nasty? How do you know him?"

Wink shrugged. "I've worked a few crews for companies where's he's been the geologist. Guy has no respect for drill crews,

220

looks down his nose at everyone. Plus, I've heard more than one rumor of his jumping claims or at least taking credit for work done by other geologists."

Obviously I must have looked pretty astonished because Wink added quickly, "Of course, they were just rumors . . . you never know . . ."

My thoughts went racing but I couldn't concentrate because Wink asked, insistently, "So who's Ivan Thorpe?"

"Shirley Walton's new husband."

He nodded. "Yup. A man in that position could cause a lot of trouble."

"Yeah. He's also a pilot," I added dismally. "The same pilot who first flew me over Gladys's property when I was prospecting."

Wink's jaw clenched. "That ain't good."

"No. But I've got to keep my feet on the ground here. I can't go getting all weird and thinking I see bogymen behind every tree. I-T-N-F . . . hell, those letters could stand for anything — Intercontinental Testing for . . . Nonprofit Foundations . . . or, well, anything. Point is, we just don't know."

Wink leaned against the tailgate, crossed his arms over his chest and studied the ground. I began to pace. Just then the diesel engine sputtered.

Stick had shut down the drill. Mule

walked over to us, dropped a box of core at our feet and said with satisfaction, "That's the last three feet of the last core hole on this job."

"Good enough," Wink told him. "Y'all get the casing pulled and stacked. By that time the boys at the creek'll be up this way and we can all head back to Raleigh."

"Okay, Wink. Miss Cleo," Mule said tipping his hard hat to me as he returned to the rig.

"A pleasure as always, Mule. Look forward to working with you guys again real soon." I felt my cell vibrate in my pocket and checked it.

"Speak of the devil," I said to Wink, "and up he pops. Let me see what he wants."

TWENTY-ONE

"It's Friday night in the big town," said a chipper Nash Finley. "Let's go to that new Greek restaurant. Eat lots of grape leaves and drink ouzo. I'll grab a cab and pick you up. That way we don't have to watch ourselves."

"You're going have to give a girl more than a few hours' notice," I said, working hard to keep a neutral tone in the face of his jocularity. I liked that he assumed I was in Raleigh, so I decided to coddle his misperception. Thank god for cell phones. "I've got lots of work to catch up on. Plus I told Henri I'd help her run a few errands."

"Bummer," said Nash. "I was hoping we could —"

"Gotta go, Nash! Henri's trying to beep in. Call you later," I interrupted, seeing Mule pulling on his work gloves in preparation for retrieving the casing from the core hole. I didn't want Nash to hear him crank the massive diesel and give up that I was on-site, standing next to a drill rig.

Now I was even more in doubt about him. His call had brought about another realization. A bad one. A real bad one.

I walked back to where Wink had laid out the last box of core and started logging again. I needed to keep the flow of my suspicious thoughts running, so right away I said to Wink, "You know what you said about how treacherous Nash can be when it comes to taking credit for someone else's work?"

"Yeah."

"Well, normally I'm very careful not to ever say anything to anyone that would let them know where I am at any particular time on a job or what I'm doing. But, there was this one time —"

"Uh oh." Wink grimaced.

"Yeah. And the worst part of that is," I said, remembering my haste and excitement to see Nash the day he asked me to pick him up at the airport again, "it's possible he tricked me into giving him . . . well, more information than I should have."

"Like what?"

"Like I told him I was unable to see him on the weekend because I was going to the beach house to visit with Will while he was here."

Wink folded his arms over his barrel chest, waiting for an explanation.

"Don't you see?" I said. "It wouldn't have been hard to find Bud's house. Then all he had to do was watch it to see if I'd hidden Gladys there. Granted, I'm just speculating here. But if he is connected with Ivan Thorpe — and let's say he told Ivan where I'd hidden Gladys — then . . ."

"Then Ivan sent Robert Earle there to bully her into signing a Power of Attorney."

"Bingo. Only I showed up and screwed his plans."

"Are you sure Nash is the only one who could have passed that information on to Ivan?"

I didn't have to think about it. "Yep. He's the only one. If he knows Ivan."

"I'd say this proves he knows Ivan," Wink said.

I was pacing as I talked. "Even if they are partners, Ivan has more to gain, especially now that he's a member of the family."

"By that you mean, if something happened to his mother-in-law."

"Yes. And let's not forget that Ivan is the one who smokes cigarillos."

Wink gave me a questioning look.

"The day after I fell into the well and discovered Irene's body, I found some cigarillo butts behind that old house in the hayfield. Let's say someone was staking out that well, someone who smoked cigarillos. Doesn't that suggest that he knew the body was down there? That therefore he's the killer?"

This was all beginning to look pretty scary.

"At least we know Nash isn't a killer," I added.

"Yet," Wink said.

"Huh?"

"Consider this, Cleo. If Nash and Ivan were to jump your claim, they'd have to succeed in court too. Like you said, that's a crapshoot at best. If, however, *you're* dead, there's no court fight and they can worry later about reducing the number of people sharing the money in a less noticeable way."

"Oh yeah. There's that." But I didn't feel anywhere near as collected as I sounded.

"What you need to do, girl, is stay away from those two and keep Gladys hidden until you can wrap this up. We're done here, so you're almost home free."

Yeah, exactly, I thought. *Keep Gladys hidden. Now all I have to do is* find *Gladys.*

Armed with the remainder of my test data

226

and confident in the knowledge my cores were safe and on their way to a locked warehouse at Statewide Testing, I headed back to the Morning Glory.

On the way, I called Gladys's sister in Florida to see if she'd heard from Gladys. She had not, and so she got upset. I did my best to reassure her that there was nothing to worry about.

Where the hell could Gladys be? She didn't have a key to my house in Raleigh, but, nonetheless, I called my neighbor and asked if there had been any activity — perhaps a rental car in the drive, lights on at night, whatever. But she also said no.

I got another call. My banker.

"Hey, Lonnie."

"Cleo, thought you might be interested in hearing a little story."

"Okay," I muttered. Lonnie was on my shit list, but it's never advisable to alienate the man who's about to lend you four million dollars.

"I was playing golf in a charity tournament in Charlotte yesterday. A friend of mine from a competitor bank was in my foursome. He told me he was working on an interesting small business loan of a type he'd never done before. It was a large term loan to a person wanting to open a quarry.

Naturally, this piqued my interest, especially when my friend said his client would be quarrying a rare rock type. I asked what he meant by 'rare.' He said rare in regard to its geographical location, explaining that it was rare to find granite on the coastal plain of North Carolina."

My stomach churned. I looked for a place to pull off the road as hurling up my lunch was fast becoming a possibility. I said, "Did you ask for an exact location?"

"Sure did. He said it was right between the towns of Stella and Silverdale."

The satellite space between us hummed. I couldn't speak. "You there?"

"Yeah, Lonnie. I'm here. Just thinking."

"Are you thinking that someone tapped into your deposit, maybe where it extended onto the neighboring property?"

"No, because that's not possible. Anyway, I've already bought the options on all the surrounding property to cover right-of-way needs should they arise sometime in the future. Moreover, the granite dome I'm prospecting is totally confined within one parcel of property, the one on which I have an option."

"Maybe there's another granite dome down that way somewhere?"

"Not likely. In fact, that would be a

million-to-one shot."

"Soooo, what could be happening then?"

"Tell me something," I said. "Did your friend say he'd seen the site plans and the testing data?"

"Don't know about site plans, but he did have data and he even had a sample of the rock."

I knew at that instant without a shadow of a doubt who'd snuck onto my site while the crew and I were at lunch, broken into the first box of core and stolen a hand sample. And, as for wondering if someone could have gotten a duplicate key to Wink's truck and all the test data? The answer to that was yes as well.

Nash Finley might be a salesman now, but he'd worked with Wink before and knew where his crews always kept duplicate keys for his truck. He knew which hotels the drillers and foreman used when testing in this area. All he had to do was wait until Wink went to bed, take the data from the cab of his truck, copy it, return it by morning, and no one would be the wiser.

Wink was right. He was one slick, nasty, claim-jumping bastard.

"Lonnie," I said reassuringly, "I know what's going on and you're not to worry about anything. This type of thing happens all the time. Just routine, really. I have everything under control and my presentation will be ready for Tuesday. I'll bring it to you myself Monday so you'll have extra time to look everything over."

"You're not worried?"

"No. But one more question. Do you remember the name on the option? Was it a company or an individual?"

"A company, but I don't remember the name. Something with initials."

"Uh-huh. And was it a Charlotte-based company?"

"Yeah."

I swallowed hard. Nash was from Charlotte.

Twenty-Two

A long stretch of desolate road cutting through a low marshy area presented itself just in time. I pulled over and jumped out, ran around the Jeep, and threw up.

Not only had I been duped like some amateur into giving up information I'd normally never dream of letting slip, I'd done it for sex. To satisfy my curiosity about sleeping with Nash, I'd nearly lost my life's dream.

I heaved again at the realization that I'd . . . Hell, I couldn't even bring myself to think the words. But I had to face the truth: I'd acted like a man. My face burned red with the shame of it.

What next? I straightened up and wiped my face with the tail of my T-shirt.

Wait a minute. The operative word here was *nearly*. I'd *nearly* lost my dream — but not yet. I could still fix all of this.

Never mind that Nash had copies of my

data, a lousy hand sample, and a phony option. I had the original drill data and matching cores. I had bills, statements, and a proper option all signed, dated, and waiting to be filed in the courthouse, not to mention a business plan complete with startup costs compiled by the best accountants in the mining business.

But most important, I had Gladys. That is, I would after I found her. I stood in the late afternoon heat and looked up and down the lonely two-lane road. On either side Spring Peepers and various other toads called out to the setting sun as it poured liquid gold across the western horizon. From somewhere deep in the swampy woods a great horned owl hooted.

Gladys, where are you hiding now?

A chill raced over my body as I recalled something Wink had said. That Nash could avoid a protracted legal battle if I were suddenly out of the picture. I jumped in the Jeep and gunned it for the Morning Glory.

Tulip went straight to the bathroom to drink from the eternal spring and I started to close the door but met an obstacle.

"Hi Mom," Will said, sweeping past me into the room. He sat his laptop on the desk in front of the window and pulled up a chair. "Yours is the first mining presentation I've done, so I want to run a few things by you. I think we may need to make some changes."

Still holding the door open, I said. "Uh, okay. In any case, you're a pleasant surprise. How did you get here?"

Will didn't have time to answer, because just then, Bud sauntered in and gave me a peck on the lips. "Yuk. You smell like vomit."

"Flattery'll always work," I said, closing the door. "And what may I ask are you doing here?"

"Just a friendly service call. Ex-husbands have responsibilities, you know."

"Yeah, well, my account doesn't need servicing," I said, moving past him to the bathroom to brush my teeth.

"Actually, I'm here because I brought Will," Bud said, following me. "He's going to need more time with you than he thought, right Will?"

"Right, I hope that's okay with you and since tomorrow's Saturday, I was hoping you wouldn't have to be at the site and we could get some work done here," Will answered clacking away at his computer.

"Actually, I'm done out there and I've got the last of the drill data too, so that will work out very well." Actually what I wanted to do was get out and find Gladys, but I had to face it: I had no idea where she was. I needed to put some serious thought into how to go about finding her.

"Glad that's all settled," Bud said, heading for the door. "I'll go see to a room for Will."

"I'll take care of that," I said.

"Okie dokie, then," Bud said, then stopped in the doorway with an afterthought. "I've got to run back to Wrightsville and get that railing knocked out tomorrow, but I was thinking, why don't I come back over tomorrow evening and we'll all go to the Sanitary. We haven't done that in a long time. I'll take Will back with me when we're done."

The Sanitary, as the locals refer to it, is an old landmark seafood market and restaurant on the Morehead City waterfront. The prospect of dinner there and a quiet word with Bud gave me a sudden warm and fuzzy feeling. We'd had our problems, 90 percent of which were brought about by Bud's constantly trying to protect me. Someone trying to protect me right now? Maybe not such a bad idea.

"Sounds like a plan," I said.

Will and I worked well into the night putting the computer program together. While being both interesting and challenging, however, it renewed my conviction that I'd made a smart career choice when I steered away from anything requiring daily use of a monitor and keyboard.

Saturday morning we were back at it again. Gratefully, Tulip needed periodic walks that gave me time to clear my head and think about where Gladys might be.

Finally, all the hard work and noggin-scratching paid off. By the end of Saturday, the program looked like something from Madison Avenue. True to his nature, however, Will thought a few more tweaks were necessary; we were just going over them when Bud blew back in.

I glanced up at the clock. Crap! Time had gotten away from us. "Ready for dinner?" Bud asked, smiling, looking all tan and handsome.

"Count me out," Will said. "Tulip and I are going to order in pizza and keep on working. Aren't we, girl?" Tulip beat a wholehearted tattoo with her tail.

"Uh . . ." I looked at Bud, disappointment starting to cloud his face. "Sure. Just give me thirty minutes."

I'd decided in the shower not to let myself get hung up replaying the scene of Bud and the mystery babe. I needed to let him in on my Nash Finley suspicions — minus any mention of my lack of good judgment, of course.

Bud was waiting for me in the parking lot when I finished getting ready. "Nice," he said with an appreciative sniff. "Big improvement over yesterday." I looked at Bud's even features. Picture a fifty-year-old version of the actor Edward Norton. Well, you get the idea. Not really handsome, but he had his charm.

"About yesterday," I said. "I'm glad we're going to be alone. We need to talk."

Evans Street runs along the waterfront in Morehead and during the summer season, it's always packed with visitors and locals alike. Bud managed to snag a parking spot in a lot across the street from the restaurant and by the time we were seated, I'd told him just about everything.

"Doesn't surprise me one bit," Bud said, watching a skipper nestle a sixty-foot sports fisherman into its slip with ease. "I've always known Finley was as crooked as that rattler he put in your car. I can't imagine what you ever saw in him."

"Bud, let's not go there . . ."

"Well, just remember, I thought from the get-go he might have had something to do with the snake incident."

"Actually, I remember that you wondered about it, but then, after someone shot Tulip and I got pushed into a well with a dead body in it, you thought I was being melodramatic when I suggested someone was trying to scare me off. Right?"

"Well, yeah, okay. I just couldn't believe anyone would go to such lengths to control the rights to a pile of rock. Which brings me to a question I've had ever since all these incidents started up. Just exactly how much money are we talking about if you pull this whole mess off?"

"After I pay Gladys a little over a million to exercise the option, there's a term loan that amounts to another three million. Even considering operating expenses, taxes, insurance, etc., I'll be pulling in an annual income of . . . well . . . it will be over a million, maybe more, depending on demand and the economy."

A waitress showed up, sat glasses of iced water on the table, took our orders and hustled off. "That'll be a nice little chunk of change for you," Bud said nonchalantly.

Bud's family's business is a large multinational conglomerate and as CEO, he deals with million-dollar deals on a regular basis. I, on the other hand, have heretofore only *consulted* on multimillion-dollar deals.

"Well, one man's chunk of change is another's pot of gold," I said dryly.

"Wait, I'm not minimizing your achievement. Actually, I was going to say . . ."

Bud was interrupted when a couple we knew from our married days stopped by our table. After the usual exchange of polite information — what our kids were doing, what their kids were doing, blah blah blah — they left and Bud said, "What I was trying to say was . . ."

"Forget it," I said, impatiently as the waitress returned with our drinks. "Anyway, the 'chunk of change' you referred to isn't a done deal yet."

"So what's left to do?"

I blew out a frustrated sigh. "Besides keeping Gladys out of Nash and Ivan's reach, not much but the presentation for Lonnie and the top brass from the bank. After I get their okay, I exercise the lease part of the option to test — Gladys needs to sign a few more documents concerning her royalty payments — then I file a memorandum of lease in the courthouse in Onslow County. It's the keeping Gladys away from Nash and Ivan part that is worrying me. Why doesn't she just call me? I don't understand." I sipped my wine quietly for a moment.

Bud read my thoughts, "You have to wonder. I mean, Robert Earle is dead, funeral arrangements have to be made. Why wouldn't she be at home with her daughter, unless she feels she'll still get pressure to kick you out of the equation by signing a Power of Attorney."

We watched quietly as the waitress laid out our meal. I speared a tasty fried shrimp and strained to think of where Gladys could be.

"What about relatives she could stay with?" Bud asked.

"She doesn't have many left." I said. "I've checked with her sister in Florida and her cousin is dead — remember the well? I don't know if there was anyone besides Irene . . . Hey, wait a minute!"

"What?"

"Just eat up. I think I might know where Gladys is hiding out."

Twenty-Three

The house was enveloped in darkness thanks to a fingernail moon. But within, like a lightning bug in a jar, a small glow moved from room to room.

Bud cut off the truck's engine and we sat for a moment and watched it. I lowered my window and immediately had to swat a mosquito that found my jugular.

I'd opened the window hoping to hear any noises from the house that might let me know if the person with the flashlight was, as I suspected, Gladys. I don't know what kind of noise I expected, but I was listening carefully anyway.

I felt Bud's eyes on me in the darkness, "Tell me again why you think Gladys is hiding in there?" he asked.

"Think about it. Who else needs a place to hide and would know Irene's house was empty? It would be a quiet place to mourn Robert Earle and take care of his arrangements."

"I guess that makes sense," Bud said, swatting mosquitoes too. They were fierce. "I got to know Gladys a little back at Seahaven, she seems like a genuine person. Sharp as a tack. Loaded with common sense and skills learned from a lifetime of hard work. The kind of person we'd all want as grandma or mom. It's unbelievable that at a time like this she's actually having to hide here in fear of being manipulated by her own family . . . or worse."

"At first I wasn't sure that Shirley was as deeply involved as Robert Earle apparently was, but maybe I need to rethink that. There's got to be a good reason Gladys isn't going home."

"Whatever. It's just a damn shame is all," Bud said.

"Let's go see if I'm right," I said as I reached for the door. I felt Bud's hand on my arm.

"Wait," he said. "Cleo, I want to finish what I started to say back at the Sanitary. I'm really proud of you."

I stared at Bud's silhouette. I'd been waiting for over twenty years to hear those words.

He looked out the windshield and said in a voice that was almost incredulous, "This is a very complicated deal with lots of components to it, not just the discovery, but the finances and legalities as well, and you've taken charge of every aspect. I've never known this side of you, Cleo, or appreciated the woman that you are — that you've always been."

Whether it was the intimacy of the closed truck or pent-up anxiety, my chin begin to tremble. I was thankful for the dark night as I felt Bud wrap his arm around my shoulder and pull me to him.

"Ouch," I said, when the console bumped my hip.

"Oh, your ass isn't that big," Bud said in a husky voice as he dragged me into his lap and gave me a kiss that curled my toes.

I came up for air and squiggled back across the console, saying, "Look, no flashlight in the front room now. What do you say we go around to the back door and let her know we're here?"

"Umm, okay," Bud said, clearly disappointed we weren't going to finish what he started.

The back door was ajar. Now, in the movies, this is never a good sign. I should have known there and then to go back to the truck but hell, once I found Gladys everything would be fine.

I couldn't see my hand in front of my face, and the appliances were so old that no glowing dials or digital clocks shone forth. "Gladys?" I called softly. There was no answer. But from the front of the house I heard a slight scraping noise. Like someone had bumped a table.

I started to call out again, but Bud said, "Shhhh!" and held up his hand. You know, the kind of hand signal you give a dog. Stay. Sit. I'm the man. You're the pet. I'm in charge.

So much for my being a savvy, competent woman. I watched Bud move to my left toward the living room. I waited until the darkness swallowed him up, then moved to the right down the hall toward the bedrooms.

I was feeling along the wall in the hallway when a floral scent and an open door let me know I'd found a bathroom. Ever since I was a kid, being anxious made me have to pee. Now was no different. I suppressed the urge.

Blinking in the darkness, I moved farther down the hall to the bedroom at the end, then called Gladys's name again, softly. Nothing. I felt my way back up the other side of the hallway of the small house to the spot where Bud and I had separated. Then, with arms outstretched in front of me, I baby-stepped my way into what I figured was the living room and stopped.

Something was different here. Something in the air. A slight musky scent, like cologne. I'd smelled it before. I thought back. One thing I knew: Bud does not wear cologne. I whispered his name.

He didn't answer. No one was answering me.

"Bud," I whispered again, more pointedly this time. "Damn it, where are you?"

I took a step forward and cracked my shin on a table. "Shit!" I snapped, grabbing my leg. This was ridiculous. I was tired of this game, not to mention scared. Obviously Gladys wasn't here and even if she was and was hiding because she didn't know it was me, wouldn't it make sense to let her know I was here?

I focused on a lamp barely silhouetted in a large picture window and moved to turn it on. At that instant my ears seemed to crawl back on my skull and the hair stood up on the back of my neck. All that in the nanosecond right before someone clamped a damp, smelly rag over my mouth.

An innate, primitive reaction to danger passed down to us from caveman days was enough to make me close my mouth, constrict my airways and execute a stomp to the arch of my attacker's foot that would have made a Clydesdale proud. I felt the muscles in the arm around my neck give a little, so I grabbed the arm and pulled forward with all my might.

I was pretty sure I was dealing with a man, so I wasn't really expecting to throw him over my shoulder. My mind was telling me to swing him into position so I could get the business end of my foot into his groin. Operating totally on adrenaline, my right foot shot out as if I actually knew what I was doing. Imagine my surprise when he grunted and let go.

Cries of what must have been excruciating pain were accompanied by crashing about in the darkness. I backed up, groping for a weapon of some sort.

Just then, my heels met a large object on the floor that sent me sprawling backwards. My butt hit the floor at the same time my head and shoulders hit a wall.

You know that old saying about seeing stars when you get hit on the head? It's true.

"Cleo," Bud moaned. "Are you okay?"

Jeez. I'd tripped over my ex-husband. I shook the static from my buzzing brain, felt in the darkness for him and found his face. It was sticky with blood.

"Somebody hit me from behind," he mumbled as he struggled up to lean on me.

"Shhhh!" I clamped my hand over his mouth. I felt his face again. Lips, nose, eyebrows, gash. Huge gash. Warm blood flowing freely.

The stumbling and groaning at the other side of the room had mostly stopped, reduced to a scuffle now and then, like someone trying to regain his footing. I felt lightheaded and realized I'd been holding my breath. I slipped my hand into the pocket of my white linen slacks in hopes of finding a hanky to stem the blood flow. Finding none, I reached back to the gash.

I felt Bud wince under my touch but I had no choice, I wrapped my palm around the wound and put as much pressure on it as I could. We sat like that for what seemed like an eternity but was probably only a few seconds. Then, I heard another shift on the other side of the room. Heard hands sliding along a wall. Feeling their way to our location? Looking for the light switch? I stiffened knowing I'd have to do something to fight back or we'd both die right here, right now.

Bud started to squirm under my hands. He turned his face to my ear and whispered, "Gun in my belt."

Amazing how those four little words gave

me an instant feeling of power and hope. I reached under his shirttail, and sure enough, there was his 9mm Glock.

I slipped it from his waistband after quickly wiping my bloody hand off on his shirt, then released the clip and smacked it back into place with a loud crack to let the enemy know I meant business. Then I clicked off the safety to let myself know I meant business.

The Glock rested hard in my two-handed grip. My trigger finger was at the ready, just as it had been many times on the firing range when Bud and I used to target practice for fun.

One sound, I prayed. *Just give me one sound so I can hone in on you, you creepy son of a bitch.* Then I heard it. Soft and to my left. He was moving to attack me from a different side this time.

Held straight out in a V that ended with the Glock, my arms moved with my upper body, tracking the sound like a turret-mounted tank gun. Another soft bump. Too close this time. Way too close. I fired. The sound was deafening.

I saw fire spurt from the end of the Glock. Heard a muffled thud and a suppressed exclamation. "Holy shit!" Bud said. Since we'd been sitting side by side like Siamese twins, the recoil through me had knocked him over. I'd never fired a gun inside an enclosed space before. And without ear protection? Holy cow, what a blast!

"Bud?" I called to him in the dark. I dared not move the gun from my last known target. I held it steady.

"I'm okay," he answered. "Stay down!"

I could see a little light from the direction I'd fired. Maybe light from an interior doorway to the kitchen area? I squinted in the darkness, trying to see something, anything, to let me know what to do next. I needed to help Bud, but I dared not drop my guard. Had I shot and killed or just wounded whoever it was?

I held my aim and waited. Then another sound from the kitchen area. I fired again.

"Jesus!" Bud exclaimed this time.

I held my position. A few seconds ticked past. Then I heard the unmistakable sound of a door opening at the back of the house. I waited for a few more seconds before I gave the most enormous sigh. I really hadn't wanted to kill anyone tonight.

"Wait!" Bud said pulling me back down.

Crouching, I heard a car engine in the backyard. I scrambled to the picture window just in time to see the taillights of a vehicle as it sped away on the drive. Now, for sure,

I was going to have to switch the lamp on.

When I did, I saw tables, lamps, and a wooden chair overturned. Bud was sitting with his back against the wall, holding his head, blood seeping between his fingers. I grabbed a doily from the arm of a wing chair and applied pressure to the wound right above his left eyebrow.

"Looks to me like someone hit you straight on, Bud, not from behind."

He grimaced. "No. I got whacked on the back of the noggin. I must have fallen forward and hit my head on that table over there."

"Whatever," I said. "In any case, I've got to get you to an emergency room or a doc-in-a-box ASAP." I peeked under the now-crimson doily. "It's bad, Bud. Going to leave a mark for sure."

"Aww. And spoil my rakish good looks?"

Just as I got Bud upright and made sure he could stay that way, headlights swept across the picture window, reflecting a car pulling into the drive. It screeched to a stop. I heard a car door slam and the sound of footsteps coming our way. Whoever it was, he was in a hurry.

TWENTY-FOUR

I never thought I'd be so glad to see this guy. With one arm supporting Bud, I towed him to the door.

"Hello, Sheriff," I said. "We were just leaving."

"The hell you are," he said. "Not until you explain why you're here in the house of a murder victim. And who is this man and what happened to him?"

"Bud Cooper. Her husband." Bud tried to hold out his hand.

"Ex-husband," I said, sagging under Bud's weight. "We rode by to see if maybe Gladys had holed up here, saw someone with a flashlight moving from room to room and thought it might be her. Why are you here?"

"I'll ask the questions. But for your information, I was on my way home and thinking along the same lines as you. Seemed logical she might be here. Then I saw the lights on and thought for sure it was her."

He looked around the room, "Obviously, it's not."

"Whoever was here beaned Bud on the head and tried to knock me out with chloroform —" I looked placatingly at the sheriff.

He sniffed the air. "Cordite. Do I smell cordite?"

Silence.

"Did someone discharge a firearm in here? Was someone shooting at you, Miz Cooper?"

"No. I was shooting at someone," I said. I tipped my head and looked into Bud's face. He was getting that ashen look people get right before they pass out. I turned back to Sheriff Evans, who was a lot less important than Bud.

"Look. It's obvious that whoever was here tried to do us bodily harm, so yes, I shot at him. But that's not my concern right now," I held up a bloody hand to emphasize my point. "I've got to get Bud some help. We can discuss all this later."

"I'll call for an ambulance . . ."

"No!" Bud croaked. "Cleo's taking me to a doc-in-a-box. I just need a few stitches and some aspirin. I'll be fine."

"Get going then." The sheriff pointed at me. "You call me when you're done," he said and headed for his patrol car.

■ ■ ■ ■

After several hours, thirteen stitches, and serial Lidocaine injections — which Bud insisted were much worse than getting beat about the head by a maniac in a pitch-black house of horrors — we were back at the Morning Glory Inn.

I sat down to explain some things to the law.

"We're back," I told Sheriff Evans on the phone. "If you want to drop by, you can. Or else we can meet tomorrow."

"I want to wrap this up tonight. We're about done here. Dug your two slugs from the walls and dusted for prints — again. I'll see you in a few."

"Alrighty then," I said. "Room 8, the Morning Glory."

I turned back to Will, who was just starting to calm down from helping me get Bud settled. He still looked worried, though. Tulip, sitting at his feet, looked worried too.

"Feel better, now?" I asked him. "You can even stay in here with your father, if you'd like. I would never want to get between a boy and his wounded dad. I can take Tulip to your room."

"No," Will said, looking at Bud. "It'd be

best if you stayed with him. He'll take orders from you."

"You're probably right. I can use the sofa, it turns into a sleeper. And take Tulip with you." I said, ushering the two of them out and wondering if I had time for a Jack Black — my own version of Lidocaine — before Sheriff Evans arrived. I tiptoed over to the open pocket door between the sleeping quarters and the sitting area of my room to look in on Bud. He was asleep. I gently closed the door.

I was just setting the whiskey bottle on top of the mini-fridge next to a bucket of ice when Evans knocked at the door. Politely removing his ball cap, he hooked it over the wing of a chair and plopped down with a whump.

Just as politely, I asked, "Can I get you something to drink, Sheriff? Coke? Sprite? Perrier?"

"If Perrier has alcohol in it, that'd be nice. I'm off-duty now and this late hour calls for something stronger."

"Uh, Perrier probably isn't for you, then. How about a Jack Daniel's on ice? I was just about to pour myself one."

"That'll work. Then you can tell me again why you were at Irene's."

I dropped ice into our glasses. "Like I said

before, I was looking for Gladys. I know you think the case is all wrapped up, that Robert Earle did everything. But I believe Gladys is still in serious danger — and here's why." I ran through all my new revelations about Nash Finley and how I was certain they were true.

Sheriff Evans sipped his drink pensively and listened with little response except an occasional nod. When I'd said my piece, I could see the tendons in his jaw tightening. Clearly he had something to say.

"The fact that you haven't shared any of this with me until now is of grave concern to me, Miz Cooper. But let's consider that all the things you just relayed are true. That this Finley character is in business with Shirley Walton's new husband, this Ivan Thorpe guy, that only Finley would have had the knowledge of drilling operations to steal the data necessary to file for a loan so he could take over your claim . . ." Here he paused to see if I was following his line of thought.

"Yes, Sheriff. I'm on the same page with you so far."

"And," he continued, "that only he knew you'd taken Gladys to your husband's beach house . . ."

"Yep."

He downed the rest of his drink, smacked the glass on the table and said, "Combine that with the fact that someone — someone clearly looking for Gladys — tried to either kill you or kidnap you tonight."

"Yep."

The sheriff stood, stuck his cap back on his head and walked to the door. "All those things, Miz Cooper, leave me no choice but to order you to go home. Now."

"Huh?"

"You heard me. Get out of my county and let me do my work." I could only gape at him.

"You have all you need to get your loan and execute your option, right?"

"Except Gladys! If someone finds her . . . kills her . . ."

"Quiet!" he boomed. "That's where you're going to have to rely on me. Look, I'm in total sympathy with you, Miz Cooper. Meaning, I'm on your side. I will find Gladys Walton and I will bring Ivan Thorpe and Nash Finley in for questioning. Trust me.

"But I can't do my job while I'm worried about you getting kidnapped or killed on my watch. Now go home to Raleigh and stay out of trouble until I find Gladys and call you."

With that, he opened the door, taking a few steps through it before he turned and pointed at me. "I'm serious as an open grave, Miz Cooper. I don't want you running around here right now. Go home. If I have to, I'll throw you in jail until I figure out what's going on."

TWENTY-FIVE

I sat there for a while, sipping my drink. I didn't want to admit it, even to myself, but Sonny Evans had rattled me. I poured myself another drink, swirled my finger in the ice cubes, and licked it.

I sipped until the delicious elixir was gone, then went to check on Bud.

I gave him a gentle shake.

"Ummpf," he said.

"You feeling all right? Not about to leave the planet, are you?"

"Not without you," he said, reaching for me.

"Bud? You know what the doctor said. No unnecessary physical activity, and you need to be roused every few hours. That's all I'm . . ."

I didn't get to finish my sentence. Bud had his own idea of the therapy he needed. The next thing I knew my eyes popped open and it was early Sunday morning.

Where was I? *Damnit, I did it again.* I tried to beat a hasty retreat back to the sofa in the sitting room where I could scold myself in private, but as I began to slide my feet over the edge of the bed, Bud pulled me into spoon position, nibbled my ear, and murmured, "Are you thinking what I'm thinking, babe?"

A nudge in my back told me what Bud, ever the romantic, was thinking. I said, "If you're thinking about where Gladys might be, I guess so."

"Now, now," Bud said, his breath warm against the back of my neck. "I'm sure the good sheriff can handle it, and I'm equally sure you should let him." His fingers went to my breasts, where he squeezed gently and my breath caught in my throat. "Relax babe, Gladys probably has some place she goes to be by herself. Someplace hidden that only she knows about."

Bud's left hand slid slowly down my abdomen and tried to slip between my tightly clamped thighs. I made a face. Trouble was, he couldn't see it so I pulled his hands from my body and stood up, ignoring his frustrated sigh.

"Cleo, tell me you're coming back to Raleigh with me today."

"Of course I am," I lied — for the ump-teenth time in the last several days. "Wouldn't want to upset Sheriff Evans." In fact I had an entirely different plan. Something I'd told Gladys had resurfaced in my mind when Bud used the word *hidden*. I had a hunch I knew right where Gladys was. And this time, after so many times of being wrong, I had to be right. The trick was to get to her without anyone following me.

One thing was clear. I needed to get rid of Bud. His attempt to protect me last night had nearly gotten us both killed. I worked better on my own.

"Bud," I said, gathering my scattered clothes from the floor and wadding them against my chest, "I think Will should drive you home and stay with you. Just to be on the safe side. I'll get Tulip out of the way, take her with me. I've got lots of paperwork to catch up on."

I started for the door but Bud said, "Wait. I want your word you're coming back to Raleigh. I know how you are and I don't want you coming up with some scheme. You've done everything you need to do, Cleo, and Will's almost got your presentation done. It's a waiting game now. You have no reason to stay here. This whole business is far too dangerous. What if I hadn't been there last night and you'd been the one hit on the head? God only knows where you'd be now."

"Bud, I have reports I need to finish —"

"I'm serious, Cleo. Think about how treacherous these people are. At first, neither one of us really believed anyone would go to such lengths. But now that we know they will, it's doubly stupid for you to pursue this any further when you don't have to."

Bud sat up in bed. "Please, babe. You don't need the money."

"That's easy for you to say, Bud, when you have plenty. You don't know what it's like to worry about bills, about a mortgage . . ."

He was really starting to piss me off. Best to end the conversation. "Fine. You can have your own money. I'll set aside a big old trust account for you. Anything you want."

"I don't want *your* money, Bud. That's the point — the point you never understood."

Silence.

I padded back to the bed, gently pushed him back to lay down, and gave him a peck on the forehead. "Don't forget to take your antibiotics," I said and headed for the bathroom.

I heard Will's voice through the door as I toweled dry. Bud was explaining the plan for the day. It was set. The two of them would go back to Raleigh, and I'd stay here to do my "paperwork."

"Great," I whispered to my guilty countenance in the mirror.

Twenty-Six

I was in a hurry to check out my hunch
about Gladys's whereabouts. But as I was
tying my sneakers, I heard a timid knock on
the door. Tulip crouched low on all fours, a
low growl rumbling in her throat. I slid the
curtain back and peeked out.

Shirley stood on the balcony gazing at the
garden below.

I opened the door and asked her to come
in. I could see she had been crying.

I directed her to sit in one of the wing-
backs. I figured she was here to apologize
for her attack on me, for blaming me for
Robert Earle's death. But after a few minutes of unabated snuffling, and not a word
out of her, I got impatient.

"You're not a very good advertisement for
newlywed bliss, Shirley. What's wrong, girl?"

She stared at me, looking even more
pathetic. "It's Ivan. You were right. He's got
this friend" — sniff sniff — "and he talked

Robert Earle and me into trying to get Momma to sign a Power of Attorney paper so they could take over mining her land." She stifled a sob.

Even though I was already certain I knew what had been done to Gladys by her evil spawn, it was nonetheless shocking to hear one of them admit it. I got a box of tissues from the bathroom, handed her one and said, "Who's the friend?"

"His name is Nash Finley. I don't know how Ivan knows him. But it gets worse."

Was that possible?

"They've got Momma hidden down in the root cellar, but they can't make her sign the papers. I heard them say what they're planning to do to her . . ."

"What, Shirley? What are they planning to do to her?" I shouted. I also shook her. The thought of poor Gladys in a root cellar made me want to do more than shake the silly girl, but now was not the time.

"They . . . they're going to kill her. Just 'cause they're frustrated. And they don't have any other plan. They didn't know I was listening. They were in Momma's desk messing through some papers for her signature so they can forge it."

She sobbed uncontrollably for a minute, then stopped and looked up at me. Snot was running from her nose. Her lips were swollen, her face blotchy and streaked with tears.

"I just barged right in," she continued, though now with an urgency that caused her to reach out and grab my hands. "They're real mad at me, Miz Cooper. They said now that I know about their plans, I'm just as guilty as they are, and I'd better go along. But I'm not! I didn't want anything like this to happen."

She closed her eyes, then said, "I didn't know what to do so I told them I was going out to get food. I've got to do something to save Momma, but I didn't know what, so I just started driving and ended up here."

"When was this? How long have you been gone?"

She looked at her watch. "Maybe half an hour . . . little longer."

"You're right about one thing," I said. "We're going to do something to save your mother."

"But . . ."

"Don't worry. You just do what I tell you to do."

I sat in my Jeep scratching Tulip behind the ears, waiting anxiously for Shirley's call. I was at the job site and had used one of the roads Wink had forged on the back side of the Walton property, so I didn't pass by the house.

Patience is not one of my virtues; fortunately, I didn't have to practice it for long before my cell rang. I checked the screen. Excellent.

"Everything okay, Shirley?"

"I did like you told me. I drove my car into a ditch then called Ivan and told him I couldn't get it out. I said that he should bring help. He said he'd bring Nash. I can see them coming toward me now."

"You stuck the car down in the ditch pretty good, didn't you, Shirley, so it will take them at least thirty minutes to get it out?"

"Yes, yes, I did what you said!" She started to cry again.

"Good," I said, "crying is good. Keep it up. That way you won't have to answer too many questions when they get there."

Shirley cried all the harder. I hung up.

I petted Tulip, who sensed something was up. "I'm just going to get Gladys, girl," I said. "I'll be right back." I could hear her whine after me as I trotted through the woods. I figured it was about a ten-minute jog to Gladys's house.

The door was ajar when I arrived. I

pushed it open, stepped into the foyer and listened. I called out, "Anybody home?"

Silence.

Assured both men had gone to rescue Shirley, I set out to find the root cellar. As I tiptoed into the kitchen, I found more proof that Nash and Ivan had left in a hurry: a half-eaten pizza in a box on the table. The room should have been redolent with its fragrance, instead, odors of stale beer and ripening garbage warred with each other. Dirty dishes crowded the sink. Almost gagging, I opened the door to the walk-in larder.

The rope handle was right where Shirley said it would be, nestled into a groove in a three-foot by three-foot wooden trap-door in the floor. I slipped my finger under the rope, and pulled to lift it.

It did not budge.

I looked for the problem. An old oak box about the size of a large picnic cooler was blocking the door. I strained to move it and it wouldn't budge either. I slid the top off the box and rested it against a shelf. White residue. Salt. Must be an old salt chest used back in the days when country folks used to pour copious amounts of salt on raw pork as a way of preserving it.

Removing the top of the chest had re-

266

duced its weight and I was able to shoulder it off the door so I could open it. I leaned the now-open door back against the salt chest and looked down the stairs into the black depths of what Shirley had called the root cellar. I couldn't recall any time in my life when I'd been in a root cellar and had no desire to experience one now, but seeing no alternative, I took a deep breath and stepped down.

Cool but dank, humid air surrounded me as I descended the stairs until my head was just below the level of the floor. "Gladys?" I called down softly.

I heard nothing. Why wouldn't Gladys answer me if she was down here? Obviously, she wasn't. I turned to leave and saw a light switch on a doubled floor joist to my left.

Maybe Gladys wasn't answering because she was tied up, gagged. I flipped the light switch and tentatively turned and trotted the rest of the way down into the room. At first glance, it looked to be a pretty nice space, for a root cellar anyway. It was about twenty-five by fifteen feet, had a concrete floor and nicely painted beige walls. Eight rows of shelves, each about five feet long, marched across the room. Stepping farther into the room, I quickly scanned the entire space. Gladys had a fully stocked and organized root cellar. There was one key thing missing: Gladys.

I heard what sounded like the cellar door slam shut. "What the fuck?" I muttered. Then I heard a distinctive sliding sound and my heart did a double clutch. I flew to the stairs and stared up at the closed cellar door.

Don't panic. Panic won't help anything. The door probably just fell over from where you propped it against the chest, right?

Hoping against hope, I climbed back up and gave the door a tentative one-handed push. It didn't budge. Next, I sat down on the stairs and pushed up with a bust-a-gut, two-handed, give-it-all-you-can heave. It might as well have been nailed down. I figured a salt chest would do nicely too.

I reached for my cell. Oh my god. I'd left the damn thing in the Jeep thinking it would be wise not to have it ring at an inopportune moment. Seemed kind of stupid now, since they make mute buttons for those times when you're sneaking around looking for friends bound and gagged in root cellars.

Deciding now was as good a time as any to panic, I pounded the door with both fists and called for help. When that didn't work, I let go with a stream of expletives even I didn't know were in my vocabulary, then stopped and listened.

A lone cricket chirped from somewhere in the cellar.

I descended to the bottom step and sat with a dumfounded thud. It was only a few minutes ago that I was thinking of Shirley as stupid. Obviously, I needed to reassess. Visions of me beating the living daylights out of her came to mind and gave me renewed energy to look for a way out. Just then, I heard voices from somewhere behind me. I got down and tiptoed — don't ask me why — in their direction.

At the far corner of the cellar, I stopped and listened again. The voices had stopped. I looked around. At about ceiling height, an indentation, maybe ten by twenty inches and the depth of the wall, caught my attention. Perhaps it might at one time have provided ventilation, maybe even been a window.

Stretching as far as I could, I rubbed it with my hand. The screen or glass that once had been there was now a panel of plywood, painted the same beige as the walls.

At that moment, the talking resumed, seeming as if it was only a few feet from me. Visualizing the exterior of Gladys's house I guessed I was pretty near the parking area in the back.

On a shelf next to me were a bunch of

those large Costco-sized cans of pork and beans. Very quietly I made a base of four cans, then set another three on top of that. I stepped up and leaned as close to the wall as possible. I put my ear to the plywood window.

". . . blew it last night, or we'd have had her." Ivan Thorpe's voice. No doubt about it.

"It's not like I had any help from you. But not to worry. We have her now," said a voice I wished I didn't recognize so well. My ears strained closer.

"Doesn't her coming here prove she doesn't know where Gladys is?"

"Maybe, maybe not. Either way, it's time for plan B."

"Well, for that we're going to need" —

Their words were lost in the sound of gravel crunching under shoes. They were moving away. I couldn't make out what they were saying, damn it!

I wiped cold sweat from my brow. I was pretty sure I wasn't going to like plan B.

Twenty-Seven

You know how it is when you're having a real bad nightmare and you know it's just a nightmare, but you can't make yourself wake up? Well, that's how it was for me in that cellar. Besides which, everything in my body felt dangerously loose right then, including my legs, but I resolved to remain standing. I couldn't bear to think about the alternative, plan B, which I was fairly sure could be titled "The Eliminate-Cleo-Cooper Plan for Owning Your Own Granite Quarry."

I heard the distinct sound of a car engine starting, then another, through the plywood window. I waited for a while but heard nothing more than the muffled sounds of the birds in the trees beside the parking area.

I leaned against the cool wall and laid my head in the crook of my elbow. What the fuck had I been thinking to believe one word Shirley said? What was her role in all this? It was obvious now that she was lying when she told me Ivan and Nash had just arrived to pull her out of the ditch. They had to have been here, waiting for me to walk into their trap.

On the other hand, maybe Ivan and Nash told her the story she relayed to me back at the Morning Glory and she really had come to me for help. Maybe she was still in the ditch. I straightened up and blew out a determined breath. Now wasn't the time to speculate or worry about her.

Then I thought of my dear dog waiting patiently for me, and you know what? That's when I started getting pissed off. I had to get out of here, but unless Scotty beamed me up or I suddenly discovered I could re-materialize on the other side of a wall like a ghost, I was at a loss as to how to go about that.

In desperation I struck out with both fists at the plywood window. Whoa! It shot out of its place, moist, loamy air rushed in, and I was staring at the underside of the shrubs at the back of the house. Maybe I was dealing with a couple of goobers after all. They hadn't even checked the cage to see if it would hold their quarry.

Suddenly, I felt a whole bunch better, even

given the size of the tiny opening in front of me. It didn't matter, honestly, whether or not I could fit through it; out was where I was going, and nothing could stop me. Placing one hand outside the opening and one hand on the ledge, I leaped up.

"Fuck!" My forehead made a cracking sound on the painted metal frame and there was a crash as I fell off the pork and bean cans and toppled to the floor. Additional height was called for, and right quick. I pulled more beans from the shelf to add another level to my reconstructed, fiber-rich stepstool and tried again.

This time I managed to get one shoulder and a boob out. With toes digging into the wall and somewhat resembling my pet hamster when he used to squeeze through my little-girl fingers, I oozed into the narrow space between the shrubbery and the foundation.

Very scratchy shrubbery, I might add. After waiting for my body to stop hurting and to be sure the coast was clear, I took off for the cover of the woods.

I almost cried with relief when I saw the Jeep parked right where I'd left it and Tulip in the driver's seat. I opened the door and she hopped out to pee. Even greater relief came as soon as I opened the console and wrapped my fingers around the grip of my baby nine. For good measure, I reached under the seat and removed a small stainless Ruger and a SmartCarry belly holster. (It's called a belly holster because it lies flat against your belly without being noticeable, assuming your belly is flat.) I kept it in the car for potential problems with larger wild animals — a circumstance I'd so far been lucky enough not to encounter. At this point, I figured Ivan, Nash, and maybe Shirley qualified.

Back when Bud and I were married, I'd seen the Ruger outfit while we were attending one of those outdoor hunting, fishing, and gun shows. It had been a good buy at the time, and later, after we divorced and I was feeling vulnerable, I planned to get a permit to carry concealed so I would be doubly protected while prospecting. Turned out I never had time to get the permit, so I had just tucked the little gun under the seat.

Now didn't seem like a good time to worry about permits and regulations, so I dropped my Dockers and wrapped the Velcro straps around my waist. I adjusted the gun to lie snugly against my stomach, hitched up my pants, and pulled my slightly oversized T-shirt over everything. Nothing real obvious showed. "Let's go, Tulip!" I called.

I climbed behind the wheel, still furious with myself at being duped. On the other hand, maybe it was a good thing. At least now I knew without question that they meant to harm Gladys and me, so I revised my plan to play my hunch as to her whereabouts. I was still going to play it, just with much more stealth. I would take every precaution available to me to ensure they couldn't follow me to her.

Driving out of the woods as fast as I could without ripping the undercarriage from the Jeep, I hit the hardtop and drove straight to Perdue's Garage. Was it less than a week ago that Jimmy Purdue had pulled the rig out of the creek and repaired it? Seemed like a lifetime. Sunday meant the shop would be closed, but Jimmy and Melva being God-fearing folks who put their trust in the Lord meant I'd probably find a piece of junk with a key in the ignition somewhere on their lot.

A trio of rusted pickups were parked neatly in a row against the back of the main service building. Tulip and I looked into each one in turn. Keys were in all three. All three had trailer hitches — an absolute necessity for a pickup in the South — so it was just a matter of choice: two rusty S-10s, one blue, one red; or a Ford Ranger all done up in camouflage paint.

I grabbed my purse, jammed my cell and my baby nine into my field backpack, and hopped into the Ford. Tulip sat shotgun.

"Please start," I said out loud as I turned the key. The engine sprang to life and I had a quarter of a tank of gas to boot. Sweet. Another plus: the safari-style hunting hat half-mashed under Tulip's butt was just the ticket to hide my hair.

I pulled it out from under her and poked out the crown. After a little size adjustment, I piled my hair under the cap and pulled it low over my face.

Then I saw a nasty blue work shirt wadded up on the floorboard. Looking at the name on the pocket, I thanked Ernie for leaving it there. I didn't even mind that the back of his shirt sported a large, stinky oil stain. A disguise was just another precaution to keep Nash and Ivan from following me. I was hoping my showing up in Gladys's root cellar might be proof to them that I didn't know where she was, but I wasn't taking any chances.

I buttoned the shirt with one hand as I spun the steering wheel with the other and floored the gas pedal. Gravel sprayed in a rooster tail across the parking lot when I whipped onto the highway. Captain Eddie's, the marina across the street from the beach house, was my next destination. I had a plan to find Gladys and get us both to safety, and it started there.

Forty minutes later, a little after noon, as I turned into Captain Eddie's, I caught a brief glimpse of yellow crime-scene tape fluttering in the breeze over at Seahaven. I couldn't help but wince. I'd somehow make up the damage to Bud's family's house later.

I parked in the marina lot, grabbed my backpack and purse, and set out for Henri's slip. I was familiar with her boat, since I occasionally used it just to get away for the day and fish, and the little boat was just what I needed to get to Gladys's latest hiding spot.

I pulled my newly acquired Jungle Jim hat low over my aviators and made my way to the small-boat slips at the end of the dock. Tulip trotted along close on my heels.

"Hey, Miss Cleo," Matthew Holder said as I brushed by him on the dock. So much for my disguise. "Hey, Tulip." He patted her head and gave her ears a friendly pull. Maybe I should have put the hat on Tulip.

Matthew was one of several high school

or college boys who worked at Eddie's in the summer, and though I was glad he remembered me, the timing was bad. I was in a hurry. Moreover, if I recalled correctly, this was the kid who always had some geologic question for me.

"I can't believe I'm lucky enough to run into you," he said. "I've been keeping this rock in my pocket, just in case." He whipped it out and handed it to me.

I glanced down at it, handed it right back to him and said, "It's an anthrorudite."

"Get out! That is way cool how you just know this stuff," Matthew said exuberantly. Then he scratched his head. "Wait. *Anthro* is like Latin for 'man' or something . . . and *rudite* means 'rock' or . . . uh . . . ?"

I waited for the wheels to turn in the kid's brain but decided I didn't have that much time. "It's a joke, Matthew."

Blank stare.

"It's just a piece of concrete."

"Oh, ha." He forced a chuckle. "Good one, Miss Cleo. But disappointing. I thought it was, like maybe some kind of moon rock . . ."

I patted him on the shoulder. "Take some geology courses at college. You'll enjoy it. Good to see you again." I started away, then turned back. "Say, Matthew?"

"Yo."

"I wanted to do a little fishing but it's so hot, I'm afraid it might be too much for Tulip. Would you mind dog-sitting for a few hours?"

"Hey, I'd love it. She can hang out in the tackle shop with me. Come on, girl," said Matthew, clucking at her. "I'll buy you a cheeseburger."

Tulip looked at me for approval. I gave her an okay nod and she trotted behind Matthew.

I jogged to Henri's 22-foot Jones Brothers bateau, hopped in, and laid my cap and Ernie's stinky shirt on the bow. Then I dropped my purse and backpack beside the center console and bent to retrieve the key that Henri keeps on a shelf inside.

I found it, straightened up, and was inserting the key into the ignition when the face of Nash Finley loomed into view. He was leaning against a piling, one leg crossed over the other, looking all relaxed and cool in his Puma running shoes, his polo shirt untucked over Calvin Klein shorts.

So much for my skills at disguise and slipping a tail. First Matthew recognizes me without the slightest hesitation and now Nash apparently followed me like I'd left a trail of bread crumbs. I really needed to pay more attention when watching reruns of *Magnum, PI;* he never had any of these problems. I did have to hand it to myself, though, because I showed no surprise whatsoever when I looked up and saw him.

Nash took a sip from the bottle of water he was holding and, with a playful lilt in his voice, said, "You really hurt my feelings, Cleo, leaving my little party so early."

Twenty-Eight

"Party? Is that what you call it? I call it kidnapping."

"Tisk, tisk. *Kidnapping* is such an ugly word."

"Maybe, but it certainly defines trapping someone in a root cellar and not letting them out."

"You could have left at anytime."

"I could not and you know it."

"Prove it."

"I will. I've already called the sheriff and he's on his way here right now. I'm going to tell him all about it," I lied.

"Sure you have," Nash crooned. "While we wait for him, what say we take that little trip you had planned? The one where you go get the infamous Gladys Walton." Nash pushed away from the piling and took another swallow of water.

"I'm not taking you anywhere. For that matter, I can't believe I ever let you into my

281

bed — that I ever thought of you as sexy in any way or charming when all you are is a low-life, claim-jumping, kidnapping bastard."

"Stop. You're damaging my self-esteem," he said, giving me a boyish grin. "Besides, you still think I'm sexy, and you know it. Admit it, you're feeling that tingle right now, aren't you?" His eyes dilated a little and for a horrified second I thought he was going to hop in the boat and try to kiss me. "You know . . . that tingle that makes you all warm and . . ."

"Stop right there," I said, holding my hand up. "The only thing I feel when I'm around you now is . . . nausea." His grin faded a little as he lifted his shirt discreetly to show me the Smith and Wesson .45 tucked into the waist of his shorts. I looked down the dock. No one was around. I checked the other side of the marina. A couple was loading a small cruiser with picnic coolers.

"Have it your way . . . for now," Nash sighed. "Let me tell you how the rest of the day is going to go. First, you are going to take me to Gladys. Then, it's very likely you and she will meet with an accident. So sad. There'll be no doubt who's to blame for the tragedy because so many people — the sheriff, Shirley, Ivan, even your own kids —

know you've hidden Gladys for your own financial gain." Nash slugged the last swallow from his water bottle, screwed the top back on, and pitched it into the water. The guy even *littered*. Typical.

"I tell you, Cleo," Nash said as he moved along the dock toward the bow of the boat. "If I had written it myself, I couldn't have hoped for a better ending to this saga, which I might add, would have never gone this far if you'd acted like any normal woman when faced with a rattler in her car. Or having her dog shot. Or being pushed down a well. Why didn't you just go home?"

He laughed. "Hell, even when I fixed it so the road would collapse under the rig and nearly kill your crew, you didn't back down. No, not you. Lives of the innocent mean nothing to you . . ."

He hopped down onto the bow platform of Henri's boat.

"No way," I sputtered in a rage, grabbing onto the handrail of the center console as the boat rocked with his weight. I knew from watching true crime dramas on television that you never let your abductor remove you from a public place. I had the Ruger in the belly holster, but I knew the odds of me being able to draw it quickly enough to use it were slim. I had to stall for time, keep him talking. Surely someone would walk down the dock soon.

"You've got some nerve, Nash. Talking about lives of the innocent. You, who killed Gladys's cousin thinking it was Gladys. You, who . . ."

"That wasn't me, cupcake," Nash said smoothly. "Ivan, that ignorant twit, killed the cousin. It was just a case of mistaken identity. You know, kind of like you accidentally killed that bumbling retard Robert Earle . . ."

"Don't call me cupcake. And how dare you compare an act of cold-blooded murder to what happened to me! He was trying to kill me!" Though I'd have thought it impossible, my rage ratcheted up another notch. But I'd also let him push my buttons, his obvious intention, so I resolved to shut my mouth and let him talk.

"Whatever. But, if you think about it, it works out better for all concerned, especially considering that the day isn't over." Nash's voice took on a low, sultry tone. "It could still work out. You and me. Together in business. Together in bed. Forever."

Nash moved toward me as he talked. He was holding on to the handrail on the starboard side of the center console, one foot resting on the gunwale. His arrogance was astounding. I opened my mouth to tell him so when, in the blink of an eye, he shifted his weight just enough to throw me off balance and snatch my backpack from the deck. Damnit.

He backed away from me a few steps and looked inside the bag. "Nice. I've always wanted a baby nine." He rezipped the backpack, keeping a grip on it.

In response to my best cold and stony glare, Nash touched his hand to his waist to remind me that Misters Smith and Wesson were still on duty, then backed diagonally across the boat to the port side bow and bent to open the anchor locker. Now seemed like a good time to show Nash what I thought of being together forever with him.

Henri would never be accused of being a neat freak, and her boat showed it. A coil of rope that belonged in the bow locker had been left on the deck along with the ten-pound anchor she kept in case she needed to secure the stern in a strong current. I'd kidded her many times when she added a poling platform to her boat, but she'd insisted she wanted to learn to fly cast from it. The truth was she was dating a fly fisherman at the time and probably had visions of the two of them on the platform with a good bottle of wine and a setting sun.

Fortunately for me, Henri's stiffy — the 18-foot pole used to push the boat along while standing on said poling platform — was also lying on the deck. Nash had just stepped over it to reach the forward locker and now straddled the handle end. Perfect.

I reached down, wrapped my fingers around the pole where it lay next to my left foot, and pulled straight up with all my might. Testicles must be very tender things; Nash collapsed so hard his head cracked down on the edge of the forward locker. He didn't even yell, just made this gross grunting noise, grabbed the family jewels, and curled in the fetal position.

The bad news: he'd slung my backpack with my cell and my sweet little Beretta overboard on his way down. The good news: his being stunned by the blow to his head gave me time to jam the key in the ignition. For the second time today, I prayed to the gods of the internal combustion engine.

My prayers were answered. The four-stroke woke with a purr. I hit the tilt and trim button to lower the prop and watched as Nash, his face purple with rage and pain, pushed to his knees, both hands still cradling his crotch. There were only a few seconds of incapacitation left in him and those I filled by cutting the bow and stern

286

lines with the trusty little pocketknife my brother had given me when I left home for college.

"That's twice, cupcake." Nash groaned through gritted teeth as he struggled upright. "Now it's your turn!" Holding his injured parts with one hand, he reached out with the other and lunged for me. He failed in the attempt, however; at that second, I rammed the throttle home, spun the wheel to port, and sent him bouncing off the center console's cushioned seat and over the starboard side.

I told him not to call me cupcake.

The couple loading the cruiser cursed me as I whipped out of the marina at full speed, breaking the no-wake rules and sending my Ernie shirt and cap disguise fluttering off the bow.

When I reached Motts Channel, the short channel running between Banks Channel and the Intracoastal Waterway, I pulled the throttle back enough to keep from being pulled over by a Fish and Wildlife officer. That's when, knowing my Henri like I do, I thought to check the fuel gauge. It was dead on empty. I'd never been able to teach either of my children to put a vessel away with a full tank of gas.

This wasn't good. I would need a full tank to reach my destination: my old fishing camp. The one I'd told Gladys about when I told her the story of Opal, the old woman who listened to her children and almost ended her days stuck out on a spit of limestone in an abandoned quarry. I remembered Gladys saying she knew where it was because she and Irene used to buy flowers from her.

Chugging obediently up the channel, indecision engulfed me, and not just because of the empty tank. You know how it is when one little part of a plan goes wrong and throws the whole thing into question? I'd used the boat in the first place for its stealth factor; why would Nash or Ivan think to look for me in a boat? In my mind, it was the perfect solution to keep them from following me. Now that they knew my mode of transportation, maybe it was time to change plans. What if Nash knew how to operate a boat and managed to get one? What if he'd followed me — again?

Then, gritting my teeth, I gripped the wheel and pushed indecision from my mind. I was sure my original plan was still the best option and it started with putting as much distance as possible between Nash Finley and me. But I was going to have to stop for gas. My backpack was a goner, but I still had my purse and the Bridgetender Marina was dead ahead. I pulled in and tied off at the fuel dock.

A young woman dock attendant about Matthew's age handed me the fuel nozzle and I began to fill the tank while keeping a lookout for Nash. To say that I was extremely uncomfortable being this close to where I ditched him — it takes only about fifteen minutes to navigate Motts Channel — was an understatement so I only put in ten gallons. Plenty to get me to Surf City, a safer distance away from Nash and Ivan. I'd have to fill up again, but there were plenty of marinas along the way to the cabin.

Back on the waterway, I couldn't shake the nagging worry that Gladys wouldn't be at my fish camp, though it was the only solution I could think of. It was my last hope. If she wasn't hiding there, then damned if I knew where she could be.

Twenty-Nine

Henri's boat hummed efficiently under me. I checked my watch. One o'clock Sunday afternoon and the sun beat down from a cloudless sky. Already today I'd been trapped in a root cellar and tracked down despite my best efforts. Then I was threatened with a gun by a crazy — and I do mean *crazy* — person. I was exhausted, my body burned in the sun like I was standing next to a pit fire, and I had a trip of between four and five hours ahead of me, depending on boat traffic. But there was nothing to be done for it.

I ran through the facts to reassure myself: Nash couldn't follow me if he couldn't drive a boat and in all the time I'd known him, he'd never even mentioned one. If he couldn't follow me, there was no way in hell he could know where I was headed. I wasn't even sure the county still maintained the dirt road to my cabin. The last time I'd been there, I'd had to put my Jeep in four-wheel drive to climb over two downed pine trees and slog through the mire.

With one hand on the wheel and one digging through the storage bin under my seat, I found a small, very warm bottle of water but no hat and no sunscreen. I downed the water. It might have kept me from dehydrating, but less than thirty minutes later I had to pee. At times like this, I had to admit to penis envy. And no, I couldn't hang over the side, as there were too many tourists on the waterway.

As soon as I cruised under the Surf City Swing Bridge, I swung a right into the Beach House Marina. A quick tie-up and instructions to the kid pumping gas to top off the tank, and I made for the facilities. Then, at a waterfront shop that caters to tourists, I paid a ridiculous price for a pink ball cap, which featured rhinestones spelling "Hot Stuff." What can I say? It was the cheapest one they had. I also bought sunscreen, some granola bars, and a couple more bottles of water. As I was checking out, I looked around for a phone, but saw none.

"Will that be all, Ma'am?" asked an elderly clerk with gaunt, weathered features and Ben Franklin glasses.

"Uh . . ." I hesitated, thinking of asking him if I could borrow his cell, but then who would I call? Having to confess to Bud that I'd lied to him and then ask for help? Not an option. Call the sheriff who had already ordered me to go home or risk being thrown into jail? I wasn't going there either. No doubt about it, I had to straighten all this out myself, and I could too. All I had to do was find Gladys and everything would be fine.

"Yes," I said with conviction this time as I picked up my purchases. "Yes, that will be all." I usually kept the little essentials like these in my backpack, but since that was now at the bottom of Captain Eddie's Marina, along with my gun and cell, I figured the snacks and water were prudent purchases. The thought of my baby nine becoming a home for a hermit crab brought a new stab of anger, but at least I still had the Ruger under my shirt. Having busted Nash Finley's balls almost made up for losing the Beretta. Too bad I hadn't known it was him that night at Irene's house — I'd have savored the nut crunching even more.

Back on the dock, I was surprised to see the kid was still filling the tank. I gave a quick glance at the pump. Thirty-eight gallons. Could that be right? Most boats this size have twenty-gallon tanks. Hopping in the boat, I moved to the console and checked the bubble gas gauge on the side. A little over three quarters full. Then I realized what was going on. Henri must have had a fifty-gallon tank installed as a special option. Jeez. Fifty gallons at four-fifty a gallon. No wonder she rarely filled it up.

Consoling myself with the fact that now I wouldn't have to stop more than once more in order to reach my destination, I gave the attendant my card and waited impatiently until he returned with it. He barely had time to flip my stern line inside the boat before I surged off. I turned my hot-pink cap around so it wouldn't blow off my head, opened the throttle and continued north on the ICW. With all the summer boat traffic and more no-wake zones ahead of me, it would be at least six o'clock before I reached my fish camp.

An hour later, I ripped open a granola bar and munched, then drained another bottle of water. Regardless of how much I drank, though, my mouth kept going dry because of the sick feeling in the pit of my stomach. No doubt about it. I was scared to the point of nausea. But that was a good thing, right? It kept me on my toes.

The day was windless, the water glassy —

"slick-cam," as the locals call it. Perfect for pushing the skiff to its maximum speed. Twelve miles later at ICW mile marker 246, the transverse through Camp Lejeune Marine base, I breathed a sigh of relief seeing no flashing lights warning me of bombing exercises. Besides the fact that live-fire delays could last anywhere from hours to days, a 120mm shell through the hull would put a real crimp in my plans.

Planing off on the shimmering water, marsh grass on either side a blur, I thought of the many times I'd teased Henri about her gas-guzzling, macho Honda 150 engine. Now I was glad to have it.

I soon passed Swansboro to port and then Emerald Isle to starboard as I went on and on, covering the length of Bogue Sound, slowing only for no-wake zones and barges big enough to crunch the skiff into splinters. At the Turning Basin at the Port of Morehead City, I caught another lucky break — no container ships to slow my progress. The US70 bridge hummed with beach traffic as I passed under it then turned to port and headed north up Adams Creek to the Neuse River.

The hoarse squawk of a great blue heron rising from the marsh startled me as I left the creek and glided onto the Neuse. I looked back, making sure Nash wasn't behind me. Even though I didn't know if he could pilot a boat, it had become obvious that he was a pretty resourceful bastard. Not at all the happy-go-lucky type I'd pegged him for.

Traffic on the river picked up as I drew nearer to New Bern's historic waterfront on my port side. I swept under the Neuse River Bridge, past Union Point Park, past the pre-Revolutionary homes along the river. At Bridgeton Harbor Marina, realizing I was running on fumes, I pulled over to fill up again and use the facilities. Only about fifteen or twenty minutes to go.

Marsh Island, smack in the middle of the Neuse River, just down from the abandoned quarry was a tricky place to navigate. Shoals, small fingers of sand, reaching out from the island shift constantly so I needed to be mindful of one of the most important rules of boating: don't go where the birds are walking. Now at a reduced speed, I flipped my cap back around for the ump-teenth time to further reduce the glare from the water.

I took the left fork beside the island, past the Hatteras yacht-building plant and then throttled down even more almost to an idle. The depth gauge showed enough water to support the boat, since the tide, which had been against me most of the way, was now on its way back in and working in my favor. I came to a small man-made canal, made a sharp turn to port and putt-putted along it until I saw what I was looking for: a break in the wall of the quarry.

The break, just the right size for a bass boat to squeeze through, allowed the Neuse River to flow into and flood the quarry, much to the delight of local fishermen.

I eased the boat between the sharp rocks projecting from the wall on either side of the break and began to weave my way across the 500-acre lake. Fortunately, I knew where the dragline had made its deepest cuts, how they connected to one another, and where the debris piles were. The sun angled low, burning my face under the brim of my cap and dancing in dazzling sparkles on the water, all but obscuring the shoreline. Not ideal conditions, but I pushed on. I had no choice.

At a little after six o'clock, I let the boat bump lightly against the pilings holding up the dock in front of my shack. When the company ceased operations, the edges of the quarry had been graded on a 2:1 slope to the 40-foot dropoff point, in accordance with state and federal regulations. Perfect for a dock. I cut the engine and tied off with one of several spare lines lying higgledy-piggledy on the deck.

The old weathered shack beckoned peacefully in the dappled light that filtered through the branches of century-old live oaks. It was surrounded by a small yard — a clearing really, not much grass — which was surrounded by maritime woods. I trotted across the backyard, up the old wooded steps to the screened-in porch, then to the back door. I looked around to make sure I wasn't being followed. No one. Just butterflies flitting through volunteer flowers in the remnants of a flower garden once tended by a woman named Opal.

The small screened-in porch looked just as it had the last time I saw it, except now the holes in the screen were larger. I reached up, ran my hand over the dusty door frame, and located my key.

I inserted it to unlock the door and started to push it open. A dry rustle sounded in the woods to my left. I made a little startled noise. Sweat trickled down my neck and back. The sound of a zillion bugs and birds suddenly stopped, reminding me of a bad horror movie. I stared deep into the woods. A busy opossum, getting a head start on his evening foraging, pushed through the undergrowth and trundled, nose down, into the yard.

Reaching under my shirt, I rubbed the butt of the little Ruger for reassurance, then stuck my head into the doorway.

Gladys sat at the broken-down kitchen table, a cup of tea poised mid-sip at her lips.

THIRTY

"Gladys," I said, with more of an edge to my voice than I intended. "Do you have any idea how worried I've been about you?"

She slowly lowered the cup and in the dwindling light, I saw her face crumple. She covered it with both hands.

"I don't think I can survive this." A ragged sob slipped from her lips. I knew the "this" she was referring to had nothing to do with our deal and everything to do with Robert Earle's death.

"I've been such a fool," she said through her fingers. "How can you ever forgive me? I've cost everyone so much. I've lost my son, my cousin . . ." She dropped her head onto her arms on the table like a kindergartner at nap time. "It's all my fault —"

"Oh, Gladys," I interrupted her, "do you really believe this is all your fault?" I dumped my purse and pulled up a chair to take her hand in mine.

She lifted her head, tears rolled down her face. I got up and looked under the sink. Thankfully an ancient roll of paper towels, still fairly pristine, resided there. I snapped one from the roll and handed it to her.

She blew her nose and rose to pitch the towel in the trash can under the sink. I leaned back against the counter. "I just don't know what to think anymore," she said. "I know my children are spoiled rotten, but . . . but I just can't believe they're vicious."

How could I tell her all the horrible truths I was now in possession of regarding the late Robert Earle and Ivan the Terrible? And what about Shirley? I still wasn't sure where she stood in all this. For all I knew she was waiting somewhere for a call from me that I had her mom and all was well. Still, I damn sure didn't plan on calling her to test the old "fool me once" adage.

Gladys closed the cabinet door, straightened, and looked out the window. "Is that your Bud?" she said, squinting in the glare and pointing in the direction of the dock.

Shit. There was little point in looking; I knew it wasn't Bud. It had to be Nash. I whipped around and looked anyway. "Shit," I said aloud this time. "It's Nash." How did this guy do it?

"Who?"

"It's a long story. Just believe me when I say that trouble has now arrived at our door and if we don't do something fast, he'll come right in and shake our hands like he's your best friend. Where's your car?" I called over my shoulder as I ran to the front of the house — the only other room — and looked out the window. I didn't see one. "How'd you get here?"

"Taxi partway. Road was out, so I walked the rest."

"Crap."

I ran back into the kitchen. Nash had secured his boat — a fancy yellow Key West he'd probably stolen — to the dock. It was smaller than Henri's, around eighteen feet. He looked at the house, flipped out his cell, and made a call. I could tell by his arm motions that he was giving someone directions. What the hell?

"We're going to have to make a run for my boat, Gladys. It's our only way out of this."

"What's going on? We aren't in any real danger, are we? I mean, I'll just refuse to sign the stupid Power of Attorney and we'll leave. Simple as that."

"Come on, Gladys, you don't really be-lieve that. You came here because your com-

301

mon sense told you to. That little voice that guides us all in times of danger told you if you could just ride this out somewhere until the legalities were over, you'd be safe. Am I right?"

"No. Well, yes. I mean, I don't know. Maybe I just came here because . . . because I can't handle any more of this. I haven't even buried Irene yet and now I've got to deal with my son's funeral and . . . poor Shirley, she's helpless . . ."

"Gladys!" I shook her by the shoulders. "We haven't got time for this right now." I nodded my head in Nash's direction. "That is a very bad man. He's in league with your new son-in-law."

"Son-in-law?"

"Ivan," I said, looking back to Nash still on his cell. "He married Shirley Friday at the same time" — I hated to do it, but I had to convince her, somehow, of our imminent peril — "at the same time that Robert Earle was hiding in your room at Seahaven, waiting to ambush you and force you into signing the Power of Attorney . . . one way or another."

"You don't know that."

"Yes, I do. The sheriff told me he had the papers stuffed in his pants when he . . . fell. It gets worse . . . Nash and Ivan . . . I believe they're behind everything that's taken place."

"What? Oh my God. Shirley," Gladys said. "Shirley could be in danger."

Okay, I could go with that if it would get Gladys moving. "Absolutely right. With you out of the picture, Shirley inherits everything. She could be in serious danger, so, here's what we're gonna do."

Thirty-One

But it was too late. Ivan — clearly the recipient of Nash's arm-waving directions and boat-to-truck instructions as he followed me (God knows how) all this way over water — came waltzing right in the front door. With his four-wheel-drive truck, he had been able to overcome the rundown road. I grabbed Gladys's arm and pulled her out on the porch only to meet Nash coming across the backyard, Smith and Wesson in hand. Jeez, I just couldn't catch a break! I pulled Gladys close and said to Nash, "Nice boat. Yours?"

"No," he said, "I borrowed it." He looked at Gladys. "Well, well, well. I finally meet the object of my affection. Pleased to meet you, Gladys Walton."

"Ivan," Gladys said, turning as he approached. "What's this all about?"

"You don't need to worry about anything right now, Gladys," Ivan said. "Everything's going to be taken care of for you." He turned to Nash "What now? You're calling the shots."

"You bring Cleo with you in her boat and follow me. I'll take Gladys in mine. We'll need one to get us back here because I know a place with a very useful old boom that I think Cleo might have an encounter with in hers. It sticks up out of the water, could lay open the bottom of a boat. Even cause its occupants to be thrown overboard."

"Does that mean the together forever thing is off?"

Nash gave me a look that pretty much answered my question but just to be sure he added, "Thrown overboard with broken necks. Maybe even crushed skulls."

"Oh for God's sake, Ivan," Gladys wailed. "Give me the damn Power of Attorney. I'll sign it. I know I'll end up in a nursing home or a nut house, but nothing's worth this!"

"Too late for that now," Ivan said, promptly shoving his mother-in-law at Nash. Then he grabbed me by the ponytail and dragged me to Henri's boat. He held an eight-inch switchblade under my chin, letting the edge slide a little, just for fun. The agony of just a little cut was so intense that my knees buckled a few times. Feeling the slick, sticky warmth of what I knew was blood oozing down my chest didn't help.

Ivan sent me flying headlong into Henri's boat with a squarely planted kick to my derriere. I managed to break my fall with my arms and hands, but the jolt was still horrendous. I grabbed the gunwale, pulled myself into a sitting position on the deck and decided to stay put, biding my time.

I knew Nash's destination, though frankly, I was surprised he knew anything about the history or particulars of the pit. But then, I'd clearly underestimated him from day one. The boom he'd referred to was an old electric dragline that had been stored in the first phased-out area of the pit and protected by a man-made berm. The berm had been breached during the flooding that followed Hurricane Floyd in 1999, and the enormous piece of equipment wound up pretty much submerged.

Still, what Nash didn't know — being in sales now, no longer a practicing geologist up to date on regulations — was that the EPA would not allow the dragline to stay there, so the company had to remove it. They'd had to do it in pieces, a huge job, but they got it done.

I knew this because I was the geologist assigned to the job, unnecessarily, since it primarily required engineers and lots of horsepower. At least I knew this part of Nash's plan would be a bust. Also, time spent looking for the boom on a dragline that no longer existed was time I'd have to think of some clever way out of this fine mess I'd gotten Gladys and myself into.

It didn't take long to arrive at the spot where Nash thought he'd find the tip of the boom rising to the surface of the lake. As is usually the case in a saltwater lake that gets flushed by the tides twice a day, visibility was very good. I watched as he circled and circled, looking for it. Something was causing his Key West boat to lurch forward and sputter at idle. A sticky throttle? Loose cable? Maybe lack of experience? I strongly suspected the latter.

There was still plenty of light and from where I'd been commanded to sit — the bench seat in front of the center console — I could tell that Gladys was trying to train her attention on me without being obvious about it.

I knew she was waiting for me to signal her, but I still hadn't come up with a plan or the guts to execute one. Our boats were about fifty feet apart since Ivan was hanging back to stay out of Nash's way.

Time was running out. I couldn't overpower Ivan — he was too big — but I did have a way to equalize the situation. The trick was that I needed to be up close and personal, just not close enough for Ivan to grab me.

He was squinting, watching Nash's movements over the harsh glare the sun created on the water during its final descent into the west. Every few moments Ivan would look my way to let me know he hadn't forgotten me. I waited until his next glance at me. I turned my face to the left so I could just see him from the corner of my eye.

Soon as he turned away, I pulled my Ruger from under my shirt, whipped around the console and shot him in the leg three times. Why three times? It was a very small-caliber gun. Pop. Pop. Pop. The sound, like a very loud firecracker, cracked across the water.

Ivan squalled like a wet cat, let go of the wheel and grabbed his thigh, a look of stunned amazement on his face. "You shot me!" he screamed as he sailed overboard, helped by a generous kick in the ass from me. One good turn deserves another, don't you think?

Grabbing the controls in my sweaty hands, I swung the boat in Gladys's direction. She had heard the shots, as had Nash, and though she hesitated for a moment, she managed to dodge his grab for her and dive overboard. *Atta girl!* I gunned the engine in her direction.

I needed to reach her before Nash ran over her. He made a clumsy half-circle to where she surfaced, but she dove to avoid his boat. I aimed for the broadside of Nash's boat and T-boned him. Not a full-speed-ahead, damn-the-torpedoes kind of ram; more like a tugboat-captain-late-for-dinner kind of ram.

Nash was knocked backwards away from the console, caught the gunwale behind his knees, and went overboard. The top half of him, anyway. All I could see of him were his fingers wrapped around the gunwale and the bottom half of his legs. He was getting a spectacular dunking, so I kept up the push, hoping the water would pull him the rest of the way overboard.

"Come on, Gladys! Where are you? Come up!" I pleaded out loud, watching for her head to emerge and continuing to push the Key West sideways.

About that time, Nash managed to pull himself up and dig his Smith and Wesson from his waistband. Uh-oh. I threw the boat into reverse and ducked behind the console. Three shots struck the windshield and the console. A couple of feet lower and — well, that's where the gas tank was located. I didn't want to think about that.

Just then I heard a faint voice call out a few feet behind my boat. Still shielding myself, I backed toward it. Soon as Gladys's head came level with the transom, I let go of the controls. Praying I wouldn't feel a bullet sink into my back, I fished her out.

"Stay down!" I ordered as I gently laid her on the deck. Then I hit Nash again with another midship ram. A bone-jarring one this time. For the second time in little more than three hours, I heard Nash grunt like a hog before being pitched headlong overboard, gun and all.

The thing about "borrowing" boats? You need to know something about them. Me, I'd been on the water every summer since I was a kid. It also helps if you're familiar with the territory you're boating in, especially if you're going to engage in a twilight chase. I decided to use my experience to our advantage as I motored away from Nash.

A few minutes later he had made it back on board, from the sound of the engine on the Key West. But I was ready.

Heading for a place Henri and Will used to call Shark Mountain when they were little, I was leading Nash onto my turf. The kids had named it that because back in the days when this was a working quarry, not a lake, I would bring them out after work to hunt for fossilized shark's teeth in the spoil piles of limestone marl. Besides being the hottest spoil pile in the pit for finding the ebony-black teeth, it was the highest.

After the pit was flooded, the top of the pile still breached the surface at low tide. At high tide, it was submerged by about a foot. Henri's boat, a flat-bottom bateau, drew five inches of water when on plane and hauling ass. The Key West, however, was a V-hull and would need at least fourteen inches of clearance at all times.

They say nine inches can be a girl's best friend. I was about to test that theory.

Years of calculating reserves from every conceivable location along the lip of the quarry had given me the ability to know my exact location in the pit from the configuration of the quarry wall. I looked up at the silhouette of the tree line on the far wall of the quarry and smiled. I was right on course. I flipped on my running lights. "Come on, you slimy piece of crap," I muttered. "Follow me."

I pushed the throttle wide open on the Honda 150 and looked back. The Key West turned in my direction. With a Yamaha

F-225 motor, it wouldn't take long for Nash to overtake me.

"Gladys?" I called. She was huddled on the deck in the stern.

She scrambled to her feet and came to me.

"You okay?"

"Yes, but that horrid man is after us again," she said, pointing back to the small red and green lights of the Key West as it gained on us.

"I want you to get down on the deck again. Go up front and hunker down in front of the console . . . You know, just in case . . ."

She moved to the bow just as I heard gunfire behind us. Apparently a Smith and Wesson will still work after being dunked in water — twice. Go figure.

"Almost there, Nash, sweetie," I said. "Just keep coming."

The surface of the flooded pit was mirror calm. At full speed, I swept over Shark Mountain with Nash right in my wake.

It's hard to describe the sound of nearly two thousand pounds of fiberglass and metal moving at fifty miles an hour makes when stopped abruptly by a large submerged pile of dirt. Suffice it to say that it's harsh . . . very harsh, especially when combined with the high-pitched whine of an outboard engine about to burn out.

Zigzagging at breakneck speeds through the narrow channels, I didn't stop until Gladys and I reached the Intracoastal Waterway. Then I pulled the boat into neutral and turned to Gladys. "You don't happen to have your cell on you by any chance?"

"Sorry. It's in my purse back at your fish camp."

"I need to call some law-enforcement official in Craven County and report what happened."

"You'll have to wait until we get home."

"Maybe I'll get lucky and get pulled by a fish dick. Then I can tell him."

We made better time on the way back to Eddie's. The wind and tides were with us, there was almost no boat traffic at night, plus I didn't have to make a gas stop so our trip back only took about four hours. But every ten minutes — all the way back — Gladys would hop up, touch me on the shoulder where I stood at the console, and say, "We've got to get to the house and find Shirley. We've got to go find Shirley." Over and over.

Good thing I thought so much of Gladys or I would have told her she sounded like a parrot on crack cocaine. As it was, I just kept giving her the same response: "Okay, Gladys. Okay."

We reached the dock at about eleven never having seen an officer of any kind. Figures. I did my best to quickly secure Henri's boat with the ropes left on board. We still had an hour-long drive, back in the direction we just came, ahead of us. I wasn't sure going back to Gladys's house was a good idea, but let's face it, Gladys had decided Shirley was nothing more than a spoiled child who wanted her cake before it was baked. I still hadn't made up my mind about her.

As I hustled up the dock after her, I glanced back at the skiff, now sporting a big frowny face on its bow and a few bullet holes in the center console. I'd have to do a lot of explaining to Henri.

The marina office was closed, the interior lit only by the drink machine and a night-light. I was a little concerned about Tulip, but it was a safe bet Matthew had taken her home with him. If my original plan hadn't been screwed up by Nash and Ivan, I'd have picked up Gladys and been back by nine o'clock at the latest, well before their closing time at ten. The marina opened at six. I'd call then.

"Where's your car?" Gladys asked when

we reached the parking area. "Because we've got to get to the house and . . ."

". . . and find Shirley. Yes, I know, Gladys. Come on, we're over here," I said, opening the door of the Ford Ranger for her

During the drive to the farm, in the quiet of the pickup, I told Gladys the complete, unabridged version of what my days had been like since I'd last seen her. Things I hadn't been able to explain shouting over the wind in an open boat. Things we both needed to consider.

"So that was the last time you saw Shirley? After you two planned to rescue me from the cellar?" Gladys said.

I nodded and said, "Yes, but why do you think she told me you were being held down there if it wasn't true? I mean, we need to think through other possibilities."

"Why? Because they told her they had me in the cellar, of course. And . . . and it's logical that they wouldn't let her go down there if she wasn't in on it. Don't you see?"

Well, she did have a point there.

"Oh my poor little girl. At least we know who's been behind all this now. I'm worried sick about her. I don't know how I'm going to break the news . . . about Ivan, I mean. I never liked him from the day she brought him home. But she did. Liked him, I mean.

Thought he hung the moon. Do you think he's dead?"

"I don't know . . . Maybe not, if he can swim and I didn't hit an artery."

THIRTY-TWO

It was after midnight when we finally arrived at Gladys's dark house. There was no sign of Shirley. One would think I would be bone-weary after the Sunday from hell, but instead I was amped. Gladys flipped on the lights. "She's probably out looking for us," she said immediately. "She's bound to be back soon though, and while we wait, know what we need?"

"A time machine to blast us a couple of days into the future?" I offered.

"Well, that too. But I actually had a little liquor in mind."

"A capital idea," I said. "I'll take care of that right after I call the sheriff."

"I'm going to look around first," Gladys said, heading up the stairs. "Maybe Shirley's just scared and hiding. Booze is in the buffet, bottom shelf. You know where the phone is."

I knew she was hoping she'd find Shirley

317

huddled in fear under her bed or in a closet, but I wasn't nearly so optimistic. I picked up the receiver of an old wall-mounted phone and started to dial the sheriff's cell number — which I now knew by heart — but the door flying open, banging against the wall, interrupted me. Shirley, supporting an ashen-faced, limping Ivan, filled the space. Despite Ivan having his arm draped over her shoulder, he clenched an open switchblade in his free hand. He slumped into her side. I thought for a minute he was holding her hostage.

Nope.

"Well, well, well," Shirley said, dumping Ivan in a chair and taking the knife from him. She pushed her smudged glasses up her nose, waved the blade menacingly at me. "Bitch, you better tell me where my mother is right now!"

I was too stunned to answer. I should have considered more seriously the possibility of Ivan making it back to shore. Apparently, he'd done it and called Shirley — maybe even from Gladys's cell phone.

"Cat got your tongue?" Shirley hissed. "I'm talking to you, stupid. Hang that phone up. Now!"

I dropped the receiver back in its hook.

Shirley turned to Ivan. He was holding his

thigh, his head laid back against the padded cushion of a chair. Then she turned back to me. "Look what you did to my husband," she said. "I swear, you just keep causing us trouble. Though, I have to admit, part of this is my fault."

"You think?" I said, my brain finally kicking into gear.

"Yeah . . ." Shirley looked over at Ivan, who was gingerly assessing the damage under a makeshift bandage. "I should have never left something as important as getting rid of you and Mother to a couple of fuck-ups like Ivan and Nash."

Ivan looked up and said soothingly, "Now, sugar, this plan can still be salvaged. There's good in every setback."

Shirley turned her icy stare back to him. "And that would be . . . ?"

I jumped in: "How about . . . it's good because now you have time to change course. I don't know the full measure of your involvement in all this insanity, Shirley, but you can still stop it."

It was as if I didn't exist. Ivan stood up, trying not to grimace, and said to Shirley, "We got one less share to divvy out. You know, no more Nash."

"Oh," Shirley said, "there's that, I guess, but now what are we going to do? Nash's plan, the one you told me about on the way home, was perfect. No one would have questioned a boating accident at night."

"But that's what I'm trying to tell you," Ivan said. "We still have that plan. We just need to patch up these little pea-shooter holes in my leg, first. Then we take Cleo and your mother back to Cleo's boat. I know what marina she keeps it at now — then take them back to the quarry and run them aground near where Nash bought it . . . Don't you see? It's even better now. It'll look like Nash was after the two of them all along and they *all* got killed in a tragic nighttime chase. Perfect."

"Hmm. I don't like the part about, you know, breaking their necks."

"That's a relief!" I blurted.

For the first time, Ivan acknowledged me. "Shut up!" he shouted, then, more gently, to Shirley, "We don't have to do that, sugar. We just knock them out, hold them under the water . . . they'll die by themselves. Easy as pie."

"I don't know," Shirley chewed a nail and pushed her glasses up again. "What if someone at the marina sees us?"

"Trust me. I've got it all figured out." When Shirley looked at him blankly, he continued, "I'll go get the boat. The marina's closed. No one will see me. There's a shopping center not far from the marina. You park the car there, herd them down to those vacant lots across the street on the sound side — you've got the knife to keep them in line — and I'll pick them up. Then you go back to the car and drive to that old house where you picked me up. You can find your way back there, can't you?"

"Of course I can," Shirley snapped. "I'm just wondering how you'd control them, what with you being injured and all, pookie."

Pookie? One minute he's a fuck-up, the next he's pookie. The woman clearly needed years of therapy.

"Of course," Ivan said impatiently. "Just because I couldn't drive my four-speed truck with a heavy-duty clutch, doesn't mean I can't steer a boat. Besides, once we get them in the boat, we wrap them in quilts, tie them up so they can't move their arms or legs. The quilts will keep the ropes from leaving marks. Then when I get them where I want them on the water, I'll use the crowbar from the car. It'll look like injuries sustained during a boating accident. Then I unwrap them and drop them overboard.

"Now here's the genius part: after I rip a hole in the boat with the crowbar, like it hit something submerged, I use one of those inner tubes in the garage to float the quilts and ropes — and help me keep afloat too — and paddle back to you. We can be back here by dawn or a little after, no sweat. Then there's no one to share all that lovely money with. It'll be just you and me, for the rest of our lives."

Shirley's eyes lit up. "Oh, Ivan!" she said, jumping up and down in girlish glee. "Maybe we can make this happen after all."

"Listen," I said, "when you two get through with your screwy plans — which happen to sound like something straight out of the loony bin, by the way — you might want to consider one tiny little thing."

Both Ivan and Shirley turned their attention to me. "What?" they said in impatient unison.

I pulled the trusty little Ruger from my tummy holster, pointed it at them, and said, "A gun trumps a knife any day. Seriously, didn't you two see *Raiders of the Lost Ark*?" Actually, I was too far from either one of them for an accurate shot, but they didn't know that.

"Oh shit! Not again," Ivan said, diving behind Shirley.

"Idiot!" shouted Shirley, knocking Ivan over and stepping on his leg in her haste to book it out of the house.

I stepped over a writhing Ivan and pointed the Ruger at his head. "Another taste of the peashooter?" I looked to my left and watched Shirley bound across the wide front porch to the stairs.

That was when I heard a thundering, scraping noise straight overhead. *What the hell?* I wondered. It sounded like something huge was sliding down the tin-covered porch roof. And it was. Just as Shirley hit the bottom step, an enormous load of laundry — wicker basket and all — hit Shirley and knocked her out, cold as a cod. Then, with my gun still pointed at Ivan, I jerked my head to the right at the sound of clattering footsteps down the stairs. A girl could get dizzy.

Gladys swept past me, out the front door, and down the steps. She kicked the laundry off Shirley, tied her "poor little girl's" hands behind her back with a long-sleeved T-shirt, then sprayed her with the garden hose. Shirley sputtered to consciousness, looked up at her mother, then lay back down in the grass and started to weep, reverting to her former persona.

Gladys gave her another shot from the hose — just for good measure. Then she looked at me and with firm resolution said,

"Tie that fool up tight and call the sheriff."

"Yes, ma'am," I said.

EPILOGUE

On the phone Gladys Walton was telling me about her latest adventure — a trip to Italy with Sister.

"That sounds marvelous," I said.

"Well, why don't you come with us on our next trip? It's been long enough since you took possession of the farm. The quarry's running now. Why don't you take off a few weeks?"

"Oh, I could never keep up with you two."

"We'll talk about it," she said. *"Ciao!"*

"Ciao," I echoed.

Tulip laid her chin on my knee. She always knew when I was blue. I stroked her silky ears and wondered why I was depressed. I had no reason to be. Gladys was happy. Shirley and Ivan had both pled *nolo contendere* and were doing time in separate prisons. I'd also heard Shirley had filed for an annulment. That pair deserved every happiness the court meted out to them, and more.

Maybe I was still sad because I had to give up on my dream of owning a quarry. Of course, I'd known it would be a tough slog. I used to do it for a living, after all. But in the years since I'd left GeoTech, the reins of government had changed hands and now a new political ideology was blowing through Washington that, well . . . let's just say it wasn't one to reward rugged individualism and entrepreneurship.

Did you know we have an environmental czar now? Not only that, but particulate emission standards — dust in the air, silt in the water — are now undefined. In other words, if there is no standard, then nothing is acceptable. How do you deal with that?

Once I got the county zoning permits, the state and federal mining permits, the EPA permits, the ATF permits (explosives make that a necessity) all submitted, including all their required flow charts and water-quality diagrams, I'd thought I was close, at least, to seeing the light at the end of the tunnel.

I was wrong. I was just getting started. I still had the Army Corps of Engineers, the United States Department of Mine Safety and Health, and OSHA to deal with, not to mention background checks on all possible employees.

One day, about eight months into the

permitting process, after having to hire two assistants on top of my lawyer and her assistant, I realized I hadn't seen the woods or felt the rain on my face or the snap of a frosty morning in all that time. Tulip was really out of shape. She'd lie around my office all day and stare at me while I worked behind my desk.

Plus, my bank notes were coming due and Lonnie was getting nervous again. In the end, I sold out to GeoTech and let their army of lawyers and EPA specialists fight the government. Tulip and I were both much happier with that decision.

So, the truth was that letting go of that dream definitely wasn't what was making me sad today.

Maybe it was the money. Instead of the millions a year I'd dreamed of making as the owner of my own quarry, I would only be getting hundreds of thousands a year in royalties. Still, in the deal I worked, my loan and Gladys were paid in full and my heirs would be financially independent into perpetuity. In fact, financial independence was the only part of my dream that did come true.

I felt as if I had just come from a funeral. What was wrong with me? There was no time, however, to ponder the question because the sound of the doorbell sent Tulip into a barking fit. Scrambling to her feet, she took off, furious that someone had managed to breach her canine security system.

"Tulip!" I called after her. "Knock it off!" From the windows in the sunroom adjoining the kitchen I could see an official-looking car . . . good ole Sheriff Sonny Evans.

There was a good chance he had come to tell me he had finally found the body of Nash Finley. Although the sheriff wasn't responsible for the search for Nash following his boating accident in the flooded quarry — different county — he had kept up with it and kept me informed. So far, neither divers nor cadaver dogs had found a trace of him.

"Sheriff Evans," I said. "What brings you to my door?"

"Sheriffs' convention in Raleigh," he said, stepping inside. "Thought I'd take the opportunity to stop by on my way home and give you some new information I just received from NCIC."

"Okay, whatever that is, I'm all ears. Have a seat."

Pulling a kitchen chair away from the table, he hooked his hat over his knee and said, "NCIC is the National Crime Information Center. I don't know how well you knew Mr. Finley, but I learned he was quite a dangerous character."

"I'm willing to believe you."

"Did you know he was a Ranger in the Army?"

"Nope. But it explains how he managed to track me without my seeing him."

"The thing is, he got a dishonorable discharge."

"I believe that too."

"You were very lucky."

"Amen to that."

Sheriff Evans unhooked his hat and stood to leave, but he seemed uneasy. "Since I've been sheriff," he said, "there have been four bodies dumped into that flooded quarry — all drug-related killings — and four bodies pulled from it. There's only the one small outlet to the river and no large carnivores in there, like alligators, to dispose of a corpse like Nash's."

I waited for his point.

"In other words, you should probably watch your back, Miz Cooper, for a while anyway."

I opened the door for him and gave him a pat on the back as he walked through. "Thanks for the warning, Sheriff."

"You're very welcome. Call me if you need me."

After he left I hopped to my feet and headed for the garage in search of my gardening tools. I felt like some yard work.

It would be a cold day in hell before I spent even a minute looking over my shoulder for a stupid creep like Nash Finley. I noticed I was feeling a little better. Must have been the adrenaline rush I got when I realized I had outsmarted a very nasty ex-Ranger.

Just as I started to step out the back door, Tulip, who had been leading the way, suddenly turned back, took a few steps past me and stopped. Then she did that dog thing, tilting her head from side to side, listening. Something only she could hear sent her into high-alert mode and she came up on her toes, straight as a pointer.

The hair on the back of my neck stood up. Maybe I had been a little hasty in dismissing the possibility that Nash was still out there somewhere. Just then, I felt a tiny change in the air pressure in the house and I knew immediately that someone had just opened a door.

My new baby nine was nestled in the console of the Jeep. Deciding that having it tucked behind my back would help curb the heebie-jeebies, I descended a few steps, but inside the garage doorway, I heard a low rumble from Tulip. I turned back just in time to see her stalk, stiff-legged, back into the house and disappear from view.

"Tulip!" I hissed. "Get back here!"

Then I heard her toenails as she skittered on the hardwood floor. Despite the intense jolt of panic that shot through me at the sound I marched back into the kitchen.

Just when you think you have gotten over something, damnit, you haven't. Things creep back up on you, and it takes less than you think to get you going.

Like a shell-shocked warrior, I got flash-backs of the sight of Nash pointing his Smith and Wesson and, most unpleasant, the vision of blood dripping down the front of my shirt.

I stopped beside the antique kitchen table, slid open the utensil drawer built into the skirt and quietly removed a knife. I hesitated a few moments, straining to hear something to give me a clue as to what I was dealing with.

Was that Tulip whimpering?

"Tulip!" I called out to her again. What the hell was going on? Where was she? My poor baby. Instantly rage that someone would hurt an innocent pet flew over me. I took off for the dinning room, knife raised.

Then, a familiar voice stopped me.

"Hey, babe, what are you up to?" Bud asked as Tulip the wonder dog, sitting at his feet, practically passed out with delight as he rubbed her ears.

"Goddamnit, Bud. You never heard of ringing a doorbell or knocking?"

"Of course I have, but why would I do that? It's just me. Jeez, you're jumpy as a squirrel. That a knife? Are you okay?"

"Considering you almost scared the pants off me, I guess I am."

Bud pulled his Ray-Bans down his nose and peered over them at my still-clad lower half. "Almost only counts with a scatter gun. Let me go out and come in again . . . take another shot at it."

I laughed in spite of myself. "You're a jerk, you know that? Sit down and tell me why you're here," I said, realizing that, for the first time in a long time, I didn't feel like I had a ten-pound weight sitting on my heart.

"Couple of reasons. Mostly just to see how the other half lives," Bud said, his head stuck in my refrigerator.

"Beer's in the door, bottom rack."

Bud cracked open a can and I realized something else: I've missed that sound. I keep beer just for him. Never touch the swill myself. Strictly wine for me, unless there's Jack Black to be had. He pulled a wine glass from the cabinet, poured a Pinot for me, and sat down on the other side of the table. I had missed that too. The way he knows what I want without asking. I sipped the wine.

Bud slugged down half his beer and said, "Man, it's hot out there."

I marveled at his ability to pick up right where we left off, as if he'd just seen me a day ago. He had been in Europe a lot recently, doing deals for his company. I had been behind a desk, struggling with government bureaucracy and working with Geo-Tech to open the quarry.

"Will and Henri told me about you getting squeezed into a sellout to GeoTech, Cleo. I'm sorry. I know how much you wanted to be a quarry owner . . . show 'em how it ought to be done and all."

"No biggie," I said. "Didn't you say you were here for a couple of reasons? In my book, that means three."

"You think a couple means three? I'll have to remember that." Bud gave me one of his wicked grins and sucked down the remainder of his beer.

He cracked open another and, having

quenched his thirst, took a polite swallow this time. "Well, I was just wondering . . ." Pausing, he seemed to be trying to collect his thoughts.

"You were wondering . . ." I prompted.

"Yeah. Well, you're rich now . . . and that is, after all, what you really wanted. In fact, I remember a conversation with you where you said that money was the only thing that would let you be yourself. First you wanted to be independent, to make your own way. Then, nothing would do but you had to be fabulously rich —"

"I'm still not fabulously rich. But what's your point?"

"I'm trying to tell you," Bud said, his exasperation showing. "I've been waiting all these years for you to get what you wanted. Now you've got it, so I'm here to ask why I'm still waiting?"

I took another sip of wine, nodded yet again, and thought back to my recent confinement behind a desk. Horrible. Then I thought back even further to my confinement as Bud's wife. A deeper shade of horrible. But that didn't mean I didn't love Bud. I did.

Problem was, I loved my life better, my independence, my career with its mental and physical challenges — prospecting in the woods, the deserts, the mountains, and the oceans of the world. God. I couldn't give that up to wait at home for him to come back from who knows where, doing god knows what.

If only there were some way . . . some place in the middle.

Bud laid his hand on my arm. "You're not coming back, are you?"

I gave him direct eye contact and told him the straight truth. "No, Bud, I'm not."

He withdrew his hand. "I didn't think you would. That brings me to my last reason for being here."

"Shoot," I said.

"I want to hire you."

I leaned back in my chair and stared at him. "For what?"

"To be the head geologist on a project I want to take on. I've been in Europe doing research, finding partners, working out details."

I tilted my chair onto its back legs. "What kind of project?"

"Natural gas exploration on the Outer Continental Shelf . . . off the coast of North Carolina. Could be big. Very big."

"Could be expensive. Very expensive."

"Hey, there's more stimulus money out there than even you could spend. All we

335

need to do is put up a few wind turbines . . . we could use those to power our deep-sea drilling . . ."

I laughed. "Maybe they'd power the security lights on the derrick — but go on. I admire your enthusiasm. As a matter of fact," I said, feeling an excitement I haven't felt since I found my granite mountain, "did you know this is one of my favorite daydreams, to find a commercially viable pocket of oil or natural gas off our coast? I've been collecting deep-sea topographic maps of the coast, all the latest data on the Manteo Prospect in the Carolina trough."

"Me too! I'll show you mine if you show me yours."

"Did you know that the Prospect is estimated to contain *five trillion* cubic feet of dry natural gas?"

"Why the hell do you think I'm interested? Of course I know that."

I looked at Bud. "Had dinner yet?"

"Any spaghetti sauce in the freezer?"

"Of course."

"How about dessert?"

"Maybe."

ABOUT THE AUTHOR

Debut author **Lee Mims** holds a master's and bachelor's degree in geology from the University of North Carolina–Chapel Hill, and she once worked as a field geologist. Lee is a member of Mystery Writers of America and Sisters in Crime. Currently a popular wildlife artist, *Hiding Gladys* is her debut novel. She lives in Clayton, N.C. Visit the author online at LeeMims.com.